More Praise for
FIRST LIGHT

"This mysterious novel uses science fiction to tell a tale about global warming and how all living things are connected." —*The Washington Post*

"This compelling, contemporary ice-age mystery introduces two engaging characters whose personal courage is tested as they discover one another's worlds as well as the truth about themselves. Thoroughly enjoyable arctic adventure." —*Kirkus Reviews*

"An exciting, engaging mix of science fiction, mystery, and adventure." —*School Library Journal*

"Peter and Thea are vividly realized. . . . Gracehope itself is sketched with sure strokes, its icy setting and matriarchal social structure fresh and believable." —*The Horn Book Magazine*

"An intriguing look at how global warming is affecting the arctic regions, deftly woven into a coming-of-age story." —*VOYA*

"Credible and absorbing. . . . Young readers will find this a journey worth taking." —*Publishers Weekly*

ALSO BY REBECCA STEAD

Goodbye Stranger

Liar & Spy

When You Reach Me

REBECCA STEAD

FIRST LIGHT

A Yearling Book

Text copyright © 2007 by Rebecca Stead
Cover art copyright © 2017 by Mary Kate McDevitt

All rights reserved. Published in the United States by Yearling, an imprint of Random House Children's Books, a division of Penguin Random House LLC, New York. Originally published in hardcover in the United States by Wendy Lamb Books, an imprint of Random House Children's Books, New York, in 2007.

Yearling and the jumping horse design are registered trademarks of Penguin Random House LLC.

Visit us on the Web! randomhousekids.com

Educators and librarians, for a variety of teaching tools, visit us at RHTeachersLibrarians.com

The Library of Congress has cataloged the hardcover edition of this work as follows:
Stead, Rebecca.
First light / Rebecca Stead.
p. cm.
Summary: When twelve-year-old Peter and his family arrive in Greenland for his father's research, he stumbles upon a secret his mother has been hiding from him all his life, and begins an adventure he never imagines possible.
ISBN 978-0-375-84017-3 (trade) — ISBN 978-0-375-94017-0 (glb)
— ISBN 978-0-307-49547-1 (ebook)
[1. Secrets—Fiction. 2. Greenland—Fiction. 3. Adventure and adventures—Fiction.]
I. Title.
PZ7.S80857Fi 2007
[Fic]—dc22
2006039733

ISBN 978-0-440-42222-8 (pbk.)

Printed in the United States of America
20
First Yearling Edition 2008

FOR MY MOTHER, DEBORAH,
WHOSE LOVING HEART COULD WARM
EVEN THE COLDEST PLACES,

AND FOR MY FATHER, DAVID,
TRUE BELIEVER

PROLOGUE

MATTIAS

GRACEHOPE

Most boys his age had never touched paper. There was little left. Paper was reserved for fine drawing and important documents. Mattias knew even before he could skate that if he were to harm any of it, if he were to crease one corner of one sheet, the consequences would be serious. But Mattias could not resist his mother's drawing table. He loved the drawers and panels that opened almost without a sound, the bright vials of dye, the immaculate brushes on their small rack, the smooth wooden box of charcoal. And although he was a very obedient boy in almost every other way, he regularly explored the contents of the table when he found himself alone with it. Mattias knew its every measure, including the shape of the black dye stain that had dried inside one drawer before he was born. And each time he approached the table, he expected to find it exactly as he had always found it before.

Today he found something new.

It was a thick paper envelope, closed but unsealed, underneath his mother's working sketches. Mattias unwound the string closure slowly, being careful to remember the length that should be left hanging when he tied it again. Inside was a square of paper unlike anything Mattias had ever seen. One side of the square glowed with an image in color, almost as if someone had frozen a moment in time and flattened it, capturing every detail. Even his mother, considered the most talented artist now alive, couldn't create anything like this. Mattias turned it carefully in his hands, holding the square by its sharp corners. It was an image of two women. Sisters, he thought. And there was something else—a glowing blur behind them.

The sun.

ONE

PETER

NEW YORK CITY

SEVEN YEARS LATER

A headache, Peter thought as he lay in bed with one arm thrown over his eyes, is something you have to experience to understand. No one can describe a headache to someone who has never had one. He rolled to one side and reached for the little spiral notebook on his night table.

Peter's mother had gotten headaches for as long as he could remember. They sometimes lasted for days, during which she sat in the red chair next to the pull-out couch where his parents slept. She didn't eat, or laugh, or make the "proper supper" she otherwise insisted upon. She hardly got up at all. "She's gone away again," his father would say. "But she'll be back." It happened maybe twice a year.

Everyone said how much Peter was like his mother—their skin that was nearly paper white, their all-over freckles, their wavy hair (hers dark, his blond like his father's), even the way they sneezed (always twice), and laughed (very quietly, after one loud sort of bark). So Peter had always assumed that, like his mother, he would get headaches one day, and that, when he did, they would be headaches just like hers.

Peter paged through the worn notebook. It had his friends' phone numbers in it, and the names of some video games he wanted if his parents ever let him *get* a video game, and the address of a company in Oregon that sold old radio parts for almost no money, and a bunch of other things. He flipped to the inside back cover, where he had made a series of slashes.

Just after his twelfth birthday, Peter's mother began asking him whether he had a headache. She had never asked him that before, and he couldn't help thinking it was strange she had to ask at all. Wouldn't it be obvious when he had a headache? Wouldn't he, too, sit in the living room and never smile or get hungry? But she kept asking, every week or two, always smiling carefully, as if she were expecting bad news. So they waited, together.

Peter got his first headache a few months later. He

knew right away what it was, and three things surprised him about it. First, it lasted only a few hours. Second, although it hurt some, he was able to eat the same salt-and-vinegar potato chips he bought after school every day. Third, he didn't tell his mother about it.

The only person he told was Miles. He and Miles had been in the same class every year since kindergarten. They knew everything about each other. For instance, Peter knew that Miles only pretended to hate the two stepsisters who lived uptown with Miles's father and stepmother. The truth was that Miles liked them, and that he liked his Monday and Friday nights at his dad's— he liked how the apartment was full of life, with friends coming and going, and teasing at dinner, and the way they always ate oranges and popcorn while they watched TV together.

And Miles knew that Peter was afraid to tell his mother about his first headache because it had brought him a little closer to knowing what he had already half-known for years: that his mother's headaches were not headaches at all, but something else entirely. Something she didn't want to talk about. Something like sadness.

Then Peter had more headaches. He took the stub of a pencil from where he had wedged it into the spiral of his little notebook and made a mark next to the others. He counted to himself, slowly.

His ninth. In a month. He replaced the notebook on

the table and rolled over so he could look through the skylight next to his bed.

Peter's family lived in two rooms, if you counted the kitchen but not the bathroom. His parents were shown the apartment by mistake—the university where his father taught had it down as a two-bedroom. But his mother had loved it on sight for its high, slanted ceiling and its enormous skylights, saying she wanted to sleep under the stars, even if you couldn't make them out very well in the city. So they had taken it, and made adjustments. One of the adjustments was the pull-out couch his parents used for a bed. Peter's loft was another.

The loft was a high, carpeted platform that stretched across one end of the living room (Peter's mother always described the living room as "thankfully rather enormous"). Although it was without doubt an uncommon room, Peter's loft held what his father would call "the usual artifacts": Along with the bed, the desk, and the bookcase, there were three shoe boxes packed with baseball cards, a few stuffed animals, and a collection of old radios, most of which Peter had rebuilt himself, or tried to.

A waist-high wooden railing looked over the living room below, but there was no ladder: Peter's father had built a flight of narrow steps inside the coat closet. And while Peter could hear anything said loudly from the living room, including "Telephone!" or "Dinner's on," the polite thing was to open the closet door and call up the stairs.

His mother nearly always used the stairs, while his father was more likely to forget and yell out to him from the living room couch. Which was why it surprised Peter, still staring out through the skylight, to hear his mother calling him from the kitchen.

"Peter?" His mother was English. When she said his name, it sounded like "Pita."

Peter rolled to his back and tried to make the sound of someone absorbed in math homework.

"Daddy called. He's canceling his office hours and coming home early. He has something to tell us. He says it's something big."

Peter sat up experimentally. The headache was almost gone now. For a moment he could see a kind of flickering from the corner of his eye, something that disappeared when he turned his head.

"How big?" he called down. But there was only the sound of water running and dishes clinking together in the kitchen sink.

Peter's father was a glaciologist. He studied glaciers. Or, as Miles liked to call them, big ice cubes. There were two parts to the job. One part was teaching in New York. Peter knew that side of his father very well: He wore V-neck sweaters with a shirt and tie underneath, had orange juice and seven-grain toast for breakfast every day, and got home by five o'clock, unless it was Wednesday, when he played basketball with some professors. Most nights, Peter could hear him clicking away on his laptop, writing an article about global warming or making notes for a lecture.

The other part of a glaciologist's job was fieldwork. Peter's father camped for weeks at a time on arctic ice, where he drove dogsleds and snowmobiles, hoisted himself up frozen walls, and fired flares to scare polar bears away. He had eaten raw seal, ridden in helicopters, and tumbled into deep cracks in the ice. Peter knew this father from stories, most of them told by graduate students who came over for dinner. They were always talking about the time Dr. Solemn had grabbed someone who almost got blown out of an old, doorless helicopter, or the time he fired a rifle over the head of a bear to save one of the dogs. It was a little like living with Clark Kent but never once getting to meet Superman.

Peter's father arrived home flushed and breathing hard, as if he had run the seven blocks from his office. He held a rolled-up newspaper in one hand, which he used to usher Peter and his mother to the living room couch, bowing theatrically. His forehead practically touched the floor.

"Oh boy," said Peter's mother, throwing Peter a look,

"it's the queen's footman." Peter sighed. The more excited his father got, the less able he was to talk normally.

Peter settled himself next to his mother on the couch while his father dragged the coffee table off to one side so he could stand right in front of them. Center stage. He cleared his throat dramatically.

Peter groaned. "Can't you just tell us for once?"

Peter's father smiled and shook his head. "It's a story."

"When *isn't* it a story?"

Still holding the rolled-up newspaper, Dr. Solemn began.

"Once upon a time, a good deal north of New York City—in Alaska, actually—the foundation of a very expensive house began to buckle. It was a large house, built over a two-year period by a wealthy philanthropist."

He looked quickly at Peter, considering. Then he added, "A philanthropist is someone who gives away a lot of his own money."

"I *know*, Dad."

"Of course. My humble apologies." His father bowed again before continuing:

"The philanthropist loved his big house, which he called his 'retreat from the real world.' He had overseen every detail of its construction—from his mansion in Beverly Hills. He designed a gigantic fireplace for the living room, big enough for a grown man to stand in. He

9

picked out the kitchen cabinets and the tile for the bathrooms. He even had a discreet little 'cell phones off' sign made out of brass and mounted next to the front door."

"Good for him," said Peter's mother. She hated cell phones.

"Oh, please," Peter said, "Dad obviously made that part up."

Peter's father ignored them. "The philanthropist stayed in his house exactly once. When he got back to Beverly Hills, his caretaker called to tell him that there was a large depression in the floor of the game room, as if something below had been trying to suck down his custom pool table."

Peter's mother made a clucking sound. "How terrible."

"Yes," said Peter's father, nodding, "truly quite terrible. The whole house had to be torn down. The philanthropist didn't even get a chance to show it to any of his friends. Naturally, he sought explanations."

"Naturally," said Peter's mother.

"Naturally. And the philanthropist was told the strangest thing: It seemed that the foundation of his house had rested on something called the permafrost, and that this permafrost had thawed. The frost was no longer perma, and this, he was told, was the fault of something called global warming."

"Global warming?" Peter's mother shook her head. "Don't believe I've ever heard of it." Peter rolled his eyes, though he was dimly aware that a year ago he would have been playing along.

"Yes, my dear," Peter's father said, now speaking as if his wife might be hard of hearing. "*Glo*-bal *warm*-ing. The notion that gasses are gathering inside the earth's atmosphere, you know. Warming the planet, melting the ice caps, and generally wreaking havoc with the balance of nature as it now exists."

He smiled. "The philanthropist, as it turned out, was quite a reader. And he began to read about global warming. He had heard the phrase before, of course, but he had never given it much thought. The more he read, the more he thought about his wonderful house, and the worse he felt. There had to be some sort of healing process, he decided. Preferably involving a lot of money."

"How much money?" Peter asked, trying to cut to the chase.

"I'm glad you asked," his father said, unrolling his newspaper and holding it out for them to read.

It was the university newspaper. Peter read the headline out loud: "Philanthropist Promises University $1.5 Million to Study Global Warming."

His mother whistled.

"Yes," said Peter's father, in his own voice. "Big money. Part of it will send me back to Greenland with a lot of state-of-the-art equipment. And there will be enough for you two to come with me."

Peter's mother stopped smiling. "Come with you?"

"Six weeks. It's March now. We can leave in April, and we'll be back before the end of May."

Peter held his breath. He would climb ice walls. He would drive a dogsled. He might get to meet Superman.

"Peter has school . . ." His mother gestured toward Peter, as if his father might have forgotten who he was.

"I know he does, Rory. But this is worth missing a few weeks of school. And you can write your book up there."

His mother groaned and closed her eyes. She hated to be reminded about the book. It was six months late already. Peter's mother was a molecular biologist—a job even harder to explain than a glaciologist's. And her book was about mitochondrial DNA, something even harder to explain than molecular biology.

Peter's mom opened her eyes and looked up at the skylights. "Why now? Why not next year? Peter will be thirteen next year. . . ."

"Things are changing in Greenland, Rory." His dad was all business now. "More quickly than we expected."

His mind was racing, but Peter said nothing. He imagined the three of them playing Monopoly in a cozy tent, a giant bowl of cookies holding down a jackpot of Free Parking cash in the middle of the board. He saw himself being towed on a sled by a bunch of fluffy white dogs. No school, his brain chanted. No school, no school, no school.

"I'm game, Dad."

"Great, Pete. I knew you'd be up for it." His father flashed him a smile, and then looked up as Peter's mom got up and went into the kitchen.

They ordered pizza, but Peter was the only one who ate it. His parents murmured on the couch, looking at maps and calendars that slowly mounted into a pile on the coffee table.

Peter called Miles at his dad's house (it was Monday).

"Whoa," Miles said when Peter told him what was going on. "Six weeks without Chinese food?"

"Hadn't thought of that," Peter said.

"I could send some down to you, maybe. Special delivery."

"Up."

"Up what?"

"Send some *up* to me—Greenland is north, dope."

"Gotcha. I see it right here on Dad's countryball. Very big island."

"Let me guess: A countryball is a globe?" Miles was always inventing new names for things. He was writing a whole fake dictionary.

"Good one, right? So when are you leaving?"

"I'm not sure. They're still talking about it."

"Not tomorrow or anything?"

"Next month, probably. We can e-mail. Dad always brings a ton of computer stuff."

"You won't recognize me when you get back," Miles said. "I'm gonna start rowing."

"Rowing what?"

"Rowing crew, dummy. Those long boats. It gives you crazy arm muscles."

Peter sighed. Miles was suddenly very into working out. He went to the gym three times a week to lift weights.

"I gotta go," Miles said. "Family time."

"Family time?"

"Dad bought a bunch of board games. Don't ask. Miles away!" This was Miles's signoff.

Peter put the phone down and heard his parents' murmuring below him. He still had a sheet of math problems to do. He hunched over the problems. Square roots and exponents; slow going. He wasn't particularly great at math, and at least half his brain was trying to hear his parents' mumbles. Once he made out his father saying, "He *is* old enough, Rory," to which his mother responded with a long "Shhhh."

Eleven to the third degree. His mind was a blank. Finally, he stood up, flopped onto his bed, and gave himself entirely to the eavesdropping.

"This is the chance we've been . . ."

". . . *know*, but what . . ."

". . . maybe –ty years? But what if things are moving even faster?"

While he listened, Peter stared through his skylight at the taller buildings across the street, where windows blinked to life as people came home and turned on their lights. He loved watching the street awaken at night. It was like watching stars emerge.

The flickering sensation from the afternoon had returned. It flapped quietly at the corner of his eye like a tiny winged insect he could scare away or allow to hover there. He stayed still.

Across the street, three top-floor windows flamed from black to yellow at the same time. "They must have shared an elevator," Peter mused. He was getting sleepy.

And then, as if someone had drawn a curtain, the buildings across the street disappeared, and he was seeing something else, watching as if it were a movie.

A little boy in pajamas sat on a big bed, cutting his own hair with a large pair of scissors. There was a roll of wrapping paper unfurled on the bed next to him, as if someone had just wrapped a present there.

The boy was absorbed by his task, his small hand jerking open and closed. The scissors looked sharp, and the boy seemed oblivious to the fact that he was coming very close to slicing off his ear. He couldn't have been older than four.

Then a woman appeared next to the bed in a robe,

toweling her wet hair with one hand. She took a moment to grasp what was going on, and then she shouted— silently, for Peter realized he could hear nothing at all— and grabbed the scissors from the boy's hand.

Peter's eyes felt hot and dry—he blinked, and his loft abruptly reappeared around him. With it came a painful roaring in his head.

His heart was pounding. Had it been a dream? He didn't think he had been sleeping. He listened for his parents, and heard the reassuring back and forth of their voices below him. He looked through the skylight, where the benign hulk of the buildings across the street looked back with a hundred friendly yellow eyes. He *must* have fallen asleep: It was dark. He was lying in bed. It was getting late.

But where had this headache come from?

The throbbing behind his eyes slowly ebbed until it disappeared completely, leaving Peter feeling light. His parents' voices went on and on. There were no further visions of big scissors or little boys, and the more he listened to his parents' whispering, scraps of sentences emerging here and there, the more he believed he had only had a dream—a dream followed by a headache.

After a long while, his parents' voices subsided and he heard the single high squeak that meant they were unfolding their bed. He reached for the notebook on the night table, made the tenth slash on the inside cover, and, after thinking about it for a moment, drew a small star next to it.

He was nearly asleep when he thought he heard the sound of paper being handled. Listening harder, he was sure of it—there was a sort of furtive crinkling. He could have sworn his parents were passing notes. In bed. In the middle of the night.

When Peter came down the next morning, they were at the kitchen table clutching their big blue mugs of coffee (his father) and tea (his mother), looking as if they hadn't slept at all, but smiling. In fact, they were practically glowing.

"So we're going?" Peter said.

His dad took his mom's hand and squeezed it.

"We're going," she said.

TWO

PETER

A month later, there were fifteen marks on the inside cover of his spiral notebook. And one star.

It had become harder to hide the headaches since Jonas—one of his father's graduate students—had come to stay with them, sleeping on the floor of Peter's loft. There wasn't a lot of privacy, but they all agreed that they'd better get used to it, since Jonas was coming to Greenland with them. And although Dr. Solemn promised that they would be living in the most amazing tent ever conceived, he never said it was big.

The Solemns' kitchen had only three chairs, so for the

past week Jonas had perched on the little white step stool during meals. It wasn't uncomfortable, he said. Peter's mother apologized every time they sat down for the first day or two, saying that it must seem terribly unwelcoming not to have an extra chair, but Jonas always smiled, ran one hand through his cropped brown hair, and said the same thing—that he wasn't brought up to feel unwelcome.

Jonas's mother was Inuit, and he was born in Greenland, where he lived until he was six. Then his family moved to Denmark so he could go to the fancy school where his father's father was headmaster. But he spent every summer in Greenland with his Inuit grandparents. Jonas told Peter, "I can *feel* at home anywhere, but I *am* at home in Greenland."

Spending a week together in the apartment had been a great way to get acquainted. Peter and Jonas built a radio together, played gin rummy, and told each other a lot of bad jokes. One night they ate three boxes of powdered doughnuts. In fact, Jonas was around so much that Peter wondered if babysitting was part of Jonas's job description. He hoped not.

Then it was their last day in New York. The living room had luggage piled everywhere and papers were strewn across the coffee table where Dr. Solemn and Jonas had been working late the night before. Peter sat at the kitchen table between his parents, eating breakfast. He was going to spend the day with Miles, and then he had to go to bed early because they were leaving for the airport at four o'clock the next morning. He grinned at Jonas across the kitchen table, then opened his mouth and showed him his wad of chewed-up bagel.

"Ah," said Jonas, pretending to swoon, "the little brother I never had."

Jonas, Peter, and his father were on their second bagels, but Peter's mother said she was too nervous to eat. Instead, she was filling out baggage tags in her impossibly beautiful handwriting, making a neat stack next to Peter's plate.

Jonas peered at them. "And I thought my grandfather had the best handwriting on the planet."

"I know," Peter said with his mouth full. "Isn't it crazy?" His own handwriting was awful. It was one of the things that his teacher wanted him to work on while he was away. Part of the "study plan."

Peter's dad raised his eyebrows at Jonas. "Really? Which grandfather is that? The one in Greenland?"

Jonas laughed. "No, the one in Denmark. He collects fountain pens. My other grandfather couldn't care less about things like handwriting. He's mostly interested in his dogs." He glanced at Peter's mother. "No offense intended."

20

She smiled without looking up from her writing. "None taken. I'm very fond of dogs as well. I think I would get along with both of your grandfathers."

Jonas reached for a third bagel. "You and not too many other people."

Peter's mom gathered the baggage tags into one hand and stood up. "Ready?" she asked Peter. She had to pick up some just-in-case medicines at the drugstore and Peter was meeting Miles for a last swim at the university pool.

"All set."

Mrs. Solemn put her tags down on the coffee table, where they caused a small avalanche of paper to slide to the floor. Peter helped her pick everything up. "There's a tag under the couch," he said, lying on his stomach and sliding one hand out. But what he found wasn't a luggage tag. It was a scrap of paper.

"What's that?" asked his mother.

"Just a receipt." Peter shoved it into a pocket and stood up. "Let's go."

Miles was waiting for him on the corner of Tenth Street, his wavy red hair stuffed under a Yankees cap. It was weirdly hot for April, and Miles wore shorts and sneakers without socks.

"Like my new cups?" he asked Peter. "My mom bought them for me yesterday."

21

Peter looked Miles up and down. "I give up," he said. "What are cups?"

Miles sighed. "Shoes. Sneakers. Get it? Like cups for your feet."

"Hmmm. Why not call them feetcups?"

"Because feetcups sounds stupid!"

Peter grinned. "But cups doesn't?"

They started walking.

Peter floated in the pool with his eyes closed while Miles swam laps. He breathed in the chlorine smell and thought "next week, all of this will seem like a dream."

Half an hour later, they emerged into the heat and glare of what could have passed for a midsummer day.

"What now?" Miles asked, jamming his cap onto his wet head.

"Fonel's!"

Ruby Fonel made her own candy and ice cream, and her tiny store was a place Peter had loved for as long as he could remember. When he was little, Ruby used to let him come into the back and see how everything was made.

They sat with their ice cream on the old green bench in front of the store window, where a faded awning created a sliver of shade. Peter watched two pigeons walking in circles in front of them, picking at bits of stale cones.

"Sorry," he told them. "Nothing for you. This is the last ice cream cone I'm going to have for a long time, and I'm eating the whole thing."

Miles talked about his plans to "row crew" and to fin-ish his fake dictionary. Peter felt his first real wrench of sadness. It's six weeks, he told himself. Just six weeks. Six weeks in a tent on the ice with his mom, his dad, and Jonas. He looked at his cone, which was soggy and had paper stuck to it, and tossed it to the pigeons after all.

"Want to come over?" he asked Miles, stomping on the cone to crush it for the birds.

"Sure."

Two women and a little boy stood next to them as they waited to cross Sixth Avenue. One side of the boy's hair was very short and sticking out oddly from the side of his head. Peter stared at him.

". . . night of Bill's birthday dinner," one of the women was saying to the other, "and the babysitter was late, so I hopped into the shower before she got there. Next time I'll wait," she said, rubbing the boy's head, "or at least I'll put the scissors away first." The women laughed and started to cross the street.

Peter was rooted to the sidewalk. He felt a quick chill run through him, although he had been complaining about the hot sun five minutes before. The muscles in his legs were jumping around in ways he hoped didn't show. Miles looked back at him from halfway across the street.

"You coming?"

Peter started walking. His legs worked, anyway. There were explanations, he told himself. He tried to think logically, like his father did. He had probably seen the boy and his mother on the street before, or maybe at the pool. They must live right around here. He must have seen them right after the boy had cut his hair, and then had a dream about them. His brain was playing with the images in his subconscious. Wasn't that what his father said dreams were? Some part of his brain had gotten stuck on the picture of the boy with his funny hair, and had spun a dream around it. And now he was seeing the boy again. They live in the neighborhood, he told himself again. It was nothing to freak out about.

But what about the shower? How could he have known that the boy's mother had been in the shower? And she had said something about going to a birthday dinner. Wouldn't that explain the wrapping paper on the bed?

They had reached the door of his building, but Peter just stood there.

"Peter?" Miles asked. "You okay?"

Peter nodded. "I'm fine."

"Are you sure?"

"Yeah."

"Sure you're sure?"

"Yes!"

"Then how about opening the door?"

"Right." Peter felt in his pocket for his keys.

Upstairs, Peter unlocked the apartment door and pushed it open.

"Whoa," Miles said.

Directly in front of them, Jonas was climbing a blue nylon rope that he had attached to the railing of Peter's loft. He was wearing an orange T-shirt and a big pair of fur pants. It was an interesting look.

"Nice pipes!" Miles said.

"He means pants," Peter said.

"You like them?" Jonas jumped down to the floor. "Polar bear."

"Really?" Miles asked.

"Yup."

"What are you doing?" Peter asked.

"I'm practicing my holds and my knots," Jonas said. "Just in case."

"In case what?"

"In case I fall into a crevasse in the ice and have to pull myself out."

"Whoa," Miles said. "What's a crevasse?"

"A big gaping hole, more or less. Want to try?" Jonas asked.

They spent almost an hour tying knots in the rope and trying to hoist themselves up. Peter was glad to see that Miles wasn't really any better at it than he was, despite all his time at the gym. In the end, they just took turns swinging from the rope and watched Jonas inventory the gear.

There were coats and jackets, fur-lined boots, four

computers, a box of CDs, special small tents called hard-weather pods to be used in a sudden storm, a breadmaker, several pairs of binoculars, a collection of sunglasses and goggles, a thick folder of maps, a box of heavy-duty flashlights (all black, except for one red one), two crates of books, and four shovels. And much, much more. A truck was coming at three o'clock to pick it all up and drive it upstate to the Air National Guard plane that would fly them to Greenland tomorrow. Most of their stuff—crates and crates of food, tables and chairs, two propane stoves, a steam drill, a bunch of solar panels and batteries, a generator, and, of course, the tents—was already up at the hangar waiting to go.

Jonas reached for a small hard plastic case next to the couch. "Can't forget this."

Miles dropped off the rope and knelt on the floor next to Jonas. "What is that?"

Jonas smiled. "A satellite phone." The case opened with a click to reveal an old-fashioned-looking phone receiver and panel full of dials. "We have to call in every morning for a weather report. And also to confirm that we haven't frozen to death or been eaten by a bear."

"Cool," Miles breathed. "No cell phone service up there, huh?"

Jonas shook his head. "No e-mail, either." Peter had been wrong about that.

"What's this?" Peter held up a soft black case that was under the coffee table.

"Medical supplies, I think. Open it."

There was a zipper that went around three sides of the case, which opened like a book. Peter found himself looking at a series of tiny knives and some plastic tubing.

"Surgical kit," Jonas said from behind him. "Don't worry, we'll probably never need that stuff."

The front door opened and Peter's parents came in with packages.

"No peeking!" Peter's mother said, making a beeline for the kitchen. She had told Peter that she was bringing him a surprise for every Friday they were in Greenland.

Jonas took out one of the hard-weather pods, which sprang to the size of a sleeping bag. Miles crawled into the tiny tent and Jonas zipped it closed. Miles pretended to be trapped. Everyone was laughing. I'm going on an adventure, Peter told himself, closing up the surgical kit.

"Before I forget, Peter, I need your keys," his father said. "I told the landlord we would leave him a set."

"Sure." Peter tossed them over.

Then it was time for Miles to go. Peter walked him downstairs, and they stood awkwardly in front of the building.

"I'll be back before school's out," Peter said finally.

Miles nodded. "Have a great time." He pretended to

punch Peter in the arm, and then started to walk down the block. After a few steps he turned around and started walking backward.

"Miles away!" he yelled.

Peter waved and reached for his keys before he remembered that he had given them to his father. Inside his pocket, his fingers felt the scrap of paper he had found under the couch after breakfast. It wasn't a receipt. Peter took it out and looked at it again.

It was a torn corner of a notebook sheet with one sentence written on it in his father's chicken-scratch scrawl: *What's the worst that can happen?*

Peter crumpled the note up and shoved it deep into his pocket. An adventure, he told himself firmly, and pushed the buzzer for his apartment.

THREE

THEA

GRACEHOPE

Thea opened her eyes and reached for the bed-clothes she had thrown off in sleep. It couldn't be time to dress, she told herself, stretching once and then turning drowsily to one side. She found herself thinking about the names of farm animals for some reason—pig, chicken, sheep, duck, cow. She must have been dreaming about them. She wondered idly if she had them wrong again—were a horse and a pig about the same size? She was fairly certain that one was meant to be somewhat bigger than the other, but she could never remember which.

The thrumming of the waterwheel began to lull her back to sleep. Slowly, two words swam up from somewhere deep in her mind and burst into Thea's consciousness. "The council!" she cried. She sat up quickly and bumped her head on the chamber's slanted ceiling.

"Ouch. Lana! *Ouch.*" She tipped herself out of bed and pulled on the fur she had laid out the night before. She could dispense with a bath—she had soaped her hair just yesterday—but there were her bracelets to put on. The clasps took at least five minutes to get right and were one of the few things she couldn't do while she skated. How late was she?

"Lana!" She picked up the fur lying on top of her trunk, shoved her legs into it, pulled it up over her shoulders, and stumbled into the greatroom with her hands full of bracelets and her skates slung over one shoulder.

"Thea." Her aunt sat at the long table, a cup of rice-water steaming in front of her.

"Why didn't you wake me?"

"I didn't wake you because I told you I wasn't going to wake you. A girl old enough to address the council is able to rouse and ready herself." But her aunt had already stood up from her seat and begun to fasten Thea's bracelets for her. "I made you a breakfast," she said.

Thea glanced down at the table. "Thank you. But owing to you I have no time to eat it."

"You can skate with it." Her aunt's strong hands

released Thea's arm, the bracelets properly clasped. "I have a feeling Mattias is still waiting for you," she said.

Thea peered into the small bowl in front of her, and then gave her aunt a look that was genuinely grateful. "Rushberries! You shouldn't have."

Lana pretended not to hear. "Today is not a day to be late, Thea. Think of all your work. You should be on your way."

Her aunt had probably been sitting at the greatroom table since first light, struggling against her instinct to wake Thea, dress her, and feed her breakfast with her old baby spoon, which, Thea knew, Lana kept wrapped in a cloth in her worktable drawer despite the fact that one was supposed to pass these things on to others.

Thea picked up the bowl in front of her and dumped the precious fruit onto the thin pancake on her plate. She rolled the pancake deftly with a practiced hand, tucking the ends in so that she wouldn't waste a drop of berry juice, then slid expertly across the smooth floor in her stockings, stopping at the thick fur mat that lay in front of the Mainway door.

Her aunt shook her head. "Someday you are going to have to start moving about like the lady you hope to become, Thea."

"So you like to inform me." Still holding the rolled-up pancake in one hand, Thea stepped into her skates and took her outerwrap from a peg.

"Wish me luck?"

Her aunt blew her a kiss. Thea blew one back, throwing her arm out in a dramatic arc that spun her around to face the Mainway door. She took a deep breath and pushed through it into the stream of skaters outside.

Thea ate her breakfast as she skated steadily down the Mainway, greeting those who caught her eye with a short wave but keeping her head down when she could. It was a busy time of day—most people had morning workposts— and she wove in and out of the skaters in an effort to reach Mattias as quickly as possible.

Mattias lived just off the fifth pass, one of the smaller pathways that led off the Mainway. Thea nearly stumbled at the turn when a younger skater abruptly slowed in front of her, but she regained her stride easily and sped down the pass to where Mattias was standing just outside his chambers with his mother, Sela. Mattias and Sela were family: Sela was first cousin to Lana, and to Thea's mother, Mai, who died when Thea was still a baby.

"Thea!" Sela said. "It's been a full fortnight since I've laid eyes on you. Losh! Look at you! You are beautiful today, Thea, truly."

Thea gave her a playful bow of thanks. Sela didn't say that Thea looked just like her mother, but Thea knew that it was true. Whoever her sire might be—and you weren't supposed to guess—he hadn't contributed much to her appearance. Thea had a portrait of her mother, drawn by Sela's talented hand, and she had grown her wavy black hair long, just the way her mother had worn hers. Although she would never acknowledge that she spent time thinking about such a thing, she hoped it looked well against the white fur she wore.

Sela caught one of Thea's arms and tugged at her sleeve, trying to pull it down. "This is a bit small." She frowned. "I might be able to put my hands on one or two that would suit you."

There was a shortage of furs, as there was a shortage of nearly everything. There had been for as long as Thea could remember.

"Loose furs make it difficult to skate," Thea said quickly. "This one is fine."

The door behind Sela opened a crack, and Mattias's little brother, Ezra, peeked out holding a half-eaten riceflat. "Thea!"

"Good morning, Ezra."

"Tomorrow's my birthday."

Thea smiled. "I remember."

"I'm going to be five."

"We know!" Mattias said. "You've been telling us for a month!" He leaned over and tickled the boy until Ezra squealed and ran back inside. "Come on, Thea. I've been standing out here for an age—I'm nearly ice."

They set off amid a torrent of good wishes from Sela.

Thea and Mattias had learned to skate together when they were two, stumbling along the backways while Lana and Sela hovered over them. They moved together now almost as one person, arms and legs swinging side by side in perfect time.

They passed most of the trip to the council chamber without talking, Thea silently rehearsing her address to the council—she had copied it out on her lightslate so many times that she could almost see the glowing words in front of her. As they neared the eighth pass, she felt rather than saw that Mattias was edging slightly to the left.

"No, Mattias," Thea said quickly. "No time."

"There *is* time."

Just off the pass, a daughter of the fourth line named Gia made risen sweetrolls early on the morning of every council day and traded them straight from the fire through her Mainway door. No one knew how she managed to collect enough rations to bake so many rolls, but no one was asking either. Gia's rolls were special, each one an airy handful that was layer upon layer of warm pastry topped with a delicate crust that was just sweet enough. A great number of council members stopped at Gia's before their regular meeting at the end of each month. Such treats were rare.

"I'll make it up to you," Thea said. "I promise. I'll get you two on the way home."

34

"The rolls are hot *now*." Slowing on his skates, Mattias looked at her pointedly.

It was true. Once cooled, the sweetrolls were hardly worth the barter. Poor Mattias, he had probably been looking forward to them for days. Thea shook her head and offered him her best look of apology. She knew he found it hard to resist.

"Two and double it next time, then," he said grudgingly as he picked up speed again.

Minutes later, the council's high double doors came into view. Mattias's smile was warm enough as he wished Thea luck and then mounted the steps to the balcony's common seats. Thea flipped up her skate blades and wove through the crowd of council members to the empty side seats reserved for citizens addressing the council. She settled into one and looked around.

The round council chamber had been carved out of the ice as part of the original settlement. Aside from the lake, it was the biggest open space Thea had ever encountered. The ceiling was thirty feet high, and it had been dyed light blue, which was supposed to be the color of the sky.

High above the heads of the council members, sculpted walls showed life-size portraits of the Settlers, marching endlessly around the chamber, flanked by the Chikchu dogs that became their companions in the cold world above. The frozen Settlers wore "determined looks of optimism," or so said Meriwether, Thea's tutor. Thea always thought the Settlers just looked weary, as if they wanted nothing more than a place to spread their tarpaulins and sleep out of the wind for a few hours. The wind, she had been taught, had been a great torment to the Settlers in the cold world.

Out of habit, Thea looked up to where her foremother, Grace, strode purposefully at the head of the pack, one hand buried in the fur of the Chikchu dog that walked beside her. In truth, Grace never even met a Chikchu: She never saw the cold world at all. But it had been Grace's idea to escape the hunters once and forever, and it was her genius that made any of it possible.

Grace had prepared for the migration for decades: She discovered how to seal ice so that it became as permanent as stone, she invented the oxygen lamps that gave them light, and she devised the waterwheel that provided their power and drew their air down from the earth's surface. It was only fitting to have her up on the wall along with those who actually made it.

Grace's granddaughter, Sarah, just twelve years old, did survive the voyage to the cold world. Later, after the Settlers had carved their new home in the ice, she bore the settlement's first child, becoming the mother of the first bloodline. Thea looked grimly down at the seven bracelets tightly clasped to her forearm. Each of them stood for a generation of daughters descended from

Sarah. The seventh bracelet stood for Thea alone: She was the last bearing daughter of the first bloodline. If she had no daughters to carry it forward, Grace's line would die with her.

It was said that the bracelets were Grace's design. They were beautiful: Lana said that their winding intricacy reminded her of something that grew from the earth, young tendrils reaching toward light and warmth. But on Thea's arm they were a burden.

The council members were settling themselves. Thea noticed a pile of boxes and red banners on a table off to one side—decorations for the Launch celebration that was just a fortnight away. She took up her silent rehearsal again. She couldn't afford to make any mistakes. Especially given her subject.

The meeting was called to order by Rowen, Thea's grandmother, who was Chief of Council. Then the Council Secretary stood to begin the recitation of the minutes of the last meeting. Although Thea kept her head directed politely toward the speaker, she quickly stopped hearing his words. She was so nervous; there was a faint roaring in her ears. She longed briefly for the waxy lump of ambergris she had left beside her bed. She liked to knead it with her fingers. Her empty right hand squeezed itself shut.

She chanced a look at Mattias, who had found a seat in the first row of the observers' balcony. Muscled his way down there, no doubt, to be sure that she could see him if she needed to. His chin was cupped in one hand, and now he wiggled his fingers ever so slightly to her.

She couldn't wave back without looking silly, but, encouraged, Thea took a deep breath. Be calm.

Rowen was gesturing for her to rise.

Thea gave an automatic smile, and then wished she hadn't. She wasn't accepting an award. And the council was no doubt scrutinizing her every movement. She schooled her face and approached the podium.

The members wore their full furs, as it was difficult to heat the enormous space. Rowen saw the cold chamber as a symbol that the council members would be no more comfortable than any citizen of Gracehope, though Thea often reflected that she didn't see her grandmother depriving herself in many other ways. She knew that Rowen took two steaming baths each day, one at first light and one just before supper, and that she drank her tea, every morning, at full concentration, while others had to choose between diluting their monthly rations or running out altogether after a fortnight. Thea's aunt Lana drank hot ricewater instead, and saved her tea for guests.

Thea scanned the chamber for a friendly face, settling on Erick, a young historian of the twelfth line. She drew a slow breath and began.

"The people who gather in this chamber each month

are among the most thoughtful and learned in our good land." A few heads nodded pleasantly at Thea.

"And this chamber itself has a great deal to teach," Thea motioned to the frozen images of the Settlers above. "It reminds us how many years ago our people elected to follow Grace to a life of peace and community."

More nods.

"And it reminds us of the hardships our ancestors bore, of the dangerous risks they took, to build this world." She pointed to the red banners that symbolized the Settlers' bloody escape from the old world.

"Now it is our turn. From the forty who lived to settle Gracehope, our people have grown to number near six hundred. The Settlers celebrated every birth. But now third births are forbidden. We need larger gardens and cropgrowth grounds. We need more chambers, where we might build a second infirmary, and craft chambers, all warmed and lighted. Imagine a Gracehope where every child is welcome, whether firstborn or fourth. That is the world the Settlers imagined for us. And that world is waiting for us, on the other side of the lake."

But the other side of the lake was far away. And there was only one way to get there.

"We know that we cannot reach the far side of the lake from Gracehope." Thea paused. Her mother had died discovering that. "But we can reach it from the surface."

Thea saw several members' eyes dart to Rowen on the

podium behind her. She pressed on. "The Settlers braved staggering hardship so that we might thrive in peace. Now it is our turn to take a risk. Let us enlarge our world, rather than diminish our people. Let us—"

"My dear Thea." She was interrupted by her grandmother's rich and resonant voice. "Please understand that, despite your youth, you have the respect of every council member here."

Rowen was looking down from her high platform directly behind Thea. Her face was close enough for Thea to realize that she was mightily displeased. But when Rowen spoke, her voice rang out with warmth. She sounded almost encouraging. "However, you must also understand that what you propose is rather grand, particularly in light of your age and station. You are, I believe, ten and four. And not yet finished with your primary studies, if I am not mistaken."

Thea pressed her lips together. Her grandmother knew full well that Thea was still in her primary studies.

"Grandmother, I do not suggest any immediate action. I propose only that the council create a committee for research, so that we may educate ourselves about the possibility of surfacing in order to extend our land." Mattias had helped her substitute the words "committee for research" for the words "team of explorers." Who could object to research?

"I have created a proposal," she continued, "which I would like to—"

"I'm afraid, Thea," Rowen interrupted, shaking her head slowly in a way that was supposed to look friendly, "that this proposal of yours is misguided. It is also quite badly timed. There is much real work to do. The physical challenge of surfacing alone would divert enormous resources." Her voice took on a harder edge. "Or have you ascertained a convenient method of tunneling to the surface? Do you suggest that each of us abandon our workposts and start digging? Have you found us a safe place to start?"

Thea drew in a quick breath at her grandmother's anger.

Rowen continued. "You seem to forget that our ancestors were driven nearly to extinction on the surface. Or perhaps you have not yet reached that point in your study of our people's history."

"Of course I know our history," Thea snapped. "Our ancestors were hunted like animals in the old world, and they followed Grace here, to settle this land. She died trying to lead her people here so that her great-grandchildren might live, and their great-grandchildren. And I urge exploration of the surface for the same reason!"

Rowen shook her head slowly, gazing down at Thea with what might have looked like sympathy. Then Rowen looked out at the council members. "Is she not like her mother? Why, she is Mai's very image." She looked back down at Thea. "I do not mean to offend, Thea. I understand why you are drawn to your mother's passion. But you have much to learn, just as she did."

Thea flushed. Her voice began to rise. "Yes, my mother believed in the expansion of Gracehope! But she is not the reason I am here today!"

This was untrue, and Thea knew it. But she didn't slow down. "Our people are preoccupied with ration-sharing, and our growers huddle together over puzzles of food production." Thea took a deep breath to calm herself, but the words just got louder. "This is not the life that Grace pursued, and we must not cling to it out of fear and ignorance!"

Thea realized too late that the words "cling" and "ignorance" were too strong. And she had turned her back to the council members—a symbol of deep disrespect—to shout up at Rowen behind her.

"Thea." Rowen spoke in a low and frighteningly even voice. "You fail to appreciate that to address the council is a privilege. I would have thought you sensible enough not to abuse the honor by bellowing at its members as if we were willful children rather than devoted citizens of our lines. Your address is concluded. We will proceed with our agenda after the formality of a vote on your motion to form a committee."

No! Thea tried desperately to think of a way to stop her. She had put so much work into her proposal. If only the council could hear what she had to say, they would see the sense in it. "Wait . . ."

"Hands?" Rowen called out. She sounded entirely bored.

Not a single hand went up. Some of the members glared at her. Erick was studying his boots. Thea couldn't bear to look at Mattias.

"Motion denied," Rowen barked. "Committee reports. We will begin with old-quarter resources."

Thea's face burned as if she had been slapped. She gave the brief bow with which the council members concluded their addresses, and stepped down to her seat, concentrating on putting one foot in front of the other. Despite the droning succession of reports that followed, her heart galloped furiously through the remainder of the meeting, powered by both shame and anger.

When the interminable meeting was finally adjourned, Thea was the first one out of the council chamber's great double doors. Mattias was already in the courtyard waiting for her. He gave Thea's arm a quick squeeze. They skated back toward the old quarter in charged silence. It was midmorning: The flat ceiling not far above their heads was set at its brightest and the Mainway was almost empty now, with most people already at their apprenticeships or workposts. Hard skating always did

Thea good when she was upset, and she could tell that Mattias had to push himself to keep up with her.

Thea's thoughts were moving quickly, too, and the more she thought, the angrier she became. Rowen had deliberately unbalanced her. Now the members of the council would surely look at her as nothing more than a spoiled child of the first line. Rowen had meant for this to happen, and Thea had allowed it.

Mattias reached out and squeezed her arm before he pushed away at the third pass, toward the waterwheel, where he was apprenticed to the chief engineer.

"Will I see you after supper?" he called over his shoulder.

She shook her head. "I'm to work tonight."

He nodded and sped away. The waterwheel supplied Gracehope's warmth and air, and few worked harder than the engineering apprentices. Mattias often had to borrow Thea's lecture notes because Chief Berling didn't consider his apprentices' primary studies any excuse for absence. Thea knew that Mattias had taken a lot of grief for missing a morning's work to attend the council meeting. She had let him down, too.

Thea had planned to go to the lake in the afternoon. She loved to sit on one of the worn benches beneath the trees and lose herself in all of that water, listening to the fishing boats bump up against the docks, and letting her eyes reach out to the invisible shore on the lake's far side. It was where she did her best imagining about the surface, where she got closest to what the sun might feel like, or the wind. It was also where she felt closest to her mother, Mai, who had lost her life in that water.

Thea put her head down and skated home in one long sprint.

Lana was at her post in the gardens, and the chambers were empty. Thea went straight to her bedchamber, where she stripped off her fur and threw it down in a heap. She kept the lightglobe dimmed and lay down on the floor in the thin tunic and leggings she wore under her fur. She wanted to cry, but her body felt hard and brittle, as if there were no water in it anywhere.

She did some breathing exercises, concentrating on the stars her aunt had etched into the ceiling when Thea was a little girl. Tinted with a dye Lana had made herself, the patterns glowed silver in the low light. She picked out a few of the constellations that Lana had copied faithfully from the star charts. Thea always had a lot of trouble at her star-pattern drills—the arrangements seemed so random to her. What was the use of knowing them at all?

Mattias, of course, knew them at a glance. He'd spent hours with Thea on this floor, trying to help her make sense of the dots over their heads. He'd also spent a lot of time explaining other things to her. "But where exactly *is* the horizon?" she'd ask. "First you tell me that it's where the earth meets the sky, and then in the next breath you confess that in truth they don't meet at all!"

Of course, Mattias hadn't seen a real horizon any more than she had, but he absorbed that sort of knowledge without effort. Lana would probably say it was because he didn't waste a lot of energy asking why he had to learn it in the first place.

When she felt more composed, Thea sat up and reached for her trunk. Opening it, she felt among the folded robes and furs for her box. It was made of rare hardwood rather than sealed ice, and was ornately carved with an image of an oak tree, the symbol of the first line. Just looking at it gave her a feeling of peace. The box had been passed down through every generation of first-line daughters. Lana had presented it to Thea on her twelfth birthday.

Inside the box was a large oval locket, carved from bone, that had belonged to her mother. Almost impossibly smooth, the thing felt warm, somehow, to the touch. Opened, the locket revealed two tiny drawings in ink. One side held a portrait of three girls—her mother and Sela, both about twelve, with Lana, perhaps fourteen, between them. The girls' faces were close, their shoulders pressed together.

The other side of the locket held a small sketch of her mother, much less detailed than the finely drawn image that faced it. A woman by then, Mai held her baby daughter close. Thea's infant head was buried in her mother's neck, only her hair visible, already in thick dark curls.

She had no memory of what it felt like to be held by her mother. She had no memory of her mother at all. Thea stared at the tiny drawing. And then, finally, she cried.

FOUR

THEA

When Lana entered the greatroom through the dock door, Thea could tell that her aunt had heard about the council meeting.

"The bread has just been delivered," Thea said quickly, nodding to the long loaves on the table, "and I'm soaking some greens for supper."

"Wonderful." Lana crossed the greatroom to her worktable and began to take little bundles of dried flower petals out of a small, coarsely woven sack. She stacked them in a pile next to her mortar and pestle.

Thea turned back to the large basin that was set deep into the counter at one end of the greatroom and stirred the dark leaves with one hand. "I'm going to wash before we eat—I didn't have a chance this morning."

She left the greens in the basin and walked over to the washing chamber, where she carefully laid her fur on a low shelf and tucked her underthings beneath it. She had set the warmer to its highest setting, hoping it might mean less heat for Rowen's bath next door. She shivered as, unclothed, she took the three steps up to the tub. Submerging herself to her shoulders, she felt so embraced by the water that she started crying again.

A few moments later, Lana appeared in a long sleeveless tunic, holding a small vial filled with a bright orange liquid. Her eyes darted to the dial on the warmer, but she said nothing, for once, about rations. Instead she held up the vial.

"I thought you might try this out for me. I've been experimenting a little . . ."

Thea saw her aunt's face register her tears. Thea didn't cry often.

"I'm certain it didn't go as badly as that." Lana sat down on the wide steps below the washtub.

"It did," Thea said, pressing her fingertips to her eyelids, "it went as badly as it possibly could have. The council thinks I'm a spoiled child, and Rowen will have her way, and has the right to be angry at me besides, at least in the eyes of absolutely everyone."

Lana's expression hardened slowly while Thea recounted the morning's words as well as she could remember them.

"You are not the person who disgraced the first line today," Lana said when Thea finished. Her aunt's face was flushed and shining in the steamy heat of the washchamber, and there was a harshness to her voice. "There will be a few who have observed that, I promise you. Meanwhile, I am going to recommend a drop of this." She held up the vial.

Lana's fine, dark hair was caught up in a loose knot, and the short collar of her tunic stood up around her long neck. Thea was reminded of Lana's beauty every once in a while, sometimes when a grower at a market stall pressed an extra something on her "for your aunt," but mostly at times like this, when Lana was angry, her cheeks red and her dark eyes flashing. She let a few drops of bright orange liquid fall into the water, and a sharp scent of herbs surrounded Thea. The bath felt almost too hot now.

"Take a deep breath and clear your mind," Lana said. "I'm going to sit with you to be sure you don't slip under. I'm not sure whether this essence induces sleep in such a concentration."

Thea felt relaxed but quite awake and clear of mind.

She tried to review the morning's events with less emotion, but could not shake the conviction that Rowen, her own grandmother, had deliberately goaded her. Why? She could only hope that Lana was right about others having seen it as well. By the time the bathwater cooled, she felt a little better.

After an early supper of greens and bread, Thea donned her fur and strapped on her skates again. It was time for work.

"You're not taking Peg?" Lana asked, gesturing behind them to the dock door, which led to the sleigh dock and the dogs' shelter. Lana always took her own companion, Aries, to the gardens with her. The dog loved the warmth of the heaters, and usually napped most of the day under the bright cropgrowth lights.

"I can't," Thea said, feeling vaguely guilty. She really should have taken Peg for a swim in the lake today, rather than feeling sorry for herself all afternoon. Peg loved to swim. "I might not be home until morning. And Peg likes to sleep in her own bed."

Lana looked up sharply. "Morning? Thea, please don't tell me you haven't met your hours."

Thea winced. She'd hoped Lana wouldn't figure out that she was cutting things close. "It isn't a problem," she said evenly. "The cycle ends tomorrow at four. I have to work nine hours before then. I have plenty of time."

If Thea didn't meet her hours before the end of the

cycle, she would lose her common privileges—her license to use the Mainway, the few "luxury" rations with which she could barter for sweets or trinkets, and her reading rights at the archive, among other things. She had never lost privileges, but had been known to get into a tight spot from time to time.

Lana's eyebrows came together. "I know you don't need to be reminded of this today, but appearances are important. And working through the night on the eve of the new cycle looks . . ."

"Lana, Dolan asked me to work late tonight. There's to be a whelping. Cassie's temperature dropped last night."

"Oh. Well, then. Her first litter, is it? I hope things go well. You'll be home in time for breakfast?"

Thea smiled. "That's depending. Did you sneak any rushberries home today?"

"Thea!" There were already too many who believed that members of the first line got special treatment, especially when it came to extra rations. As a master gardener, Lana had daily access to some of the most coveted delicacies, like rushberries, and she was especially sensitive to the rumors. Sometimes Thea thought her aunt shorted the family a little just to prove her scruples.

"I'll have you know that was a fortnight's ration you gulped down this morning," Lana said, indignant, "and it took work to save it."

"I know." Thea quickly hugged her aunt and stepped to the Mainway door. "I'll see you in the morning—for unsweetened riceflats."

Lana smiled. "We might manage half-sweet."

The Mainway pass was dimly lit now, as it was suppertime. Thea stepped onto the pass just as the door on her right was closing. Rowen's door. Her heart beat faster at just the thought of seeing her grandmother. She had better give Rowen a wide berth for a while. She wasn't sure she could be civil, and further antagonizing the Chief of Council would do her no good at all.

Before she could push off, Lana appeared in the doorway behind her.

"Thea, remember that tomorrow night we host the first-line supper. It's Ezra's birthday. No excuses. I'll need your help." Her aunt let the door close behind her.

Thea suppressed a groan. She would be dining with Rowen tomorrow night.

She reached the Mainway quickly and started off in the direction of the breeding grounds, feeling a quick stab of reproach that she hadn't spared Cassie a thought all day. The young Chikchu was one of her special charges, and Thea herself had picked Cassie's mate. Dolan thought Thea had a knack for it, and it was true that her matchmaking had produced some beautiful litters in the past twelvemonth.

When Thea arrived at the breeding grounds, Cassie was already lying in her shallow whelping box, panting. Thea stroked the dog's face, and Cassie's tail thumped a greeting.

"Another hour or two?" she called, seeing Dolan emerge from the main house and start toward her, closely followed by Norma, a good-sized black Chikchu.

Dolan nodded, carefully setting down a portable warmer near Cassie's bed. "She's doing well." Unlike his sister, Sela, Dolan was a man of few words.

Norma settled next to him: The dog never let Dolan out of her sight. Wherever he went, she was at his heels. Dolan's own Chikchu companion preferred the company of other dogs, and could usually be found sitting among those in the main house infirmary. "He loves me in his own way," Dolan always said.

Thea smiled as Dolan took a moment to rub Norma's flank. She was a troubled dog; Thea sometimes heard her whimpering in her sleep. Though Norma frequently got under his feet, Dolan never lost patience with her.

Dolan was one person who wouldn't know about the morning's council meeting, and that was a relief. He kept to himself, spending most of his time at the breeding grounds. He refused even to foster apprentices. Some of the other chiefs were juggling more than a dozen young people, but Dolan would not relent. Unlike Mattias's elite posting as one of Chief Berling's chosen engineering

54

apprentices, Thea's position was a regular workpost, with no particular honor attached to it.

She fiddled with the heater, making sure it still blew warm. They would need it when the pups came. It was new, and Thea was glad the council understood that the breeding grounds were no place to cut corners.

"Sit with Cassie until your assembly arrives," Dolan offered. "You can help me with the inventory later." He broke into a smile. "I notice you may be here a while."

Thea grinned up at the big man, who had taken a small lightslate from his pocket. He twisted a knob, and Thea's timelog glowed on its face.

"There's nowhere I would rather be," she said playfully. "For the next nine hours, anyway."

"Nine and a half."

Thea laughed. She felt so protected here, so much at ease with Dolan and the dogs, that she sometimes wished she could let go of the rest of it, let go of the idea of expansion, and surfacing, and her mother's hopes. Dolan would be more than happy to turn the place over to her, in time. Who else did the man have? But it was impossible.

While Dolan, trailed by Norma, readied the open box that would hold the newborn pups, Thea spoke to Cassie in a soothing voice, telling her what a good job she was doing.

Cassie united all of the most important Chikchu traits—

strength, intelligence, coordination, and loyalty. It had been a challenge for Thea to choose a worthy sire for her pups. She researched the Chikchu family lines for three afternoons at the archive before settling on Atlas, whose pups were known for their speed and gentle nature. The children paired with Cassie's litter would be lucky indeed, Thea thought, slipping a square of fur from a nearby stack under Cassie's head to make her more comfortable.

"Nothing's too good for Peg's sister, eh?" Dolan teased her from the door of the main house. Thea waved him off. Cassie was littermate to her own Peg, it was true, but Thea was loath to admit she had favorites.

A minute later he called again. "The assembly is arrived."

The first assembly was one of her favorite things about working at the breeding grounds. Although a council committee officially assigned each child his or her Chikchu companion, it was almost always Thea who made the introductions.

She could just make out the slight forms of the children milling about behind Dolan, one of them nearly a head taller than the others. The main house would be humming with their excitement. "It won't do to keep them waiting," she told Cassie. With a final pat, she stood and crossed the sands.

Thea knew that the taller boy was Perry. Though most everyone agreed that he was an unpleasant child, Perry had managed to play the coveted part of William at the Launch festivities two out of the past three years. Thea just didn't understand it: He had never once gotten the speeches right. She had a private theory about the boy, who bore a strong resemblance to Meriwether, Thea's tutor. Meriwether assigned the roles at Launch every year.

Of course, sires were a secret business. The women of Gracehope weren't allowed to bear the children of whomever they chose. When a woman wanted to have a child, she summoned the Angus. The Angus had a finely woven sack that she carried to her appointments, and she kept the book of sires, which told who had fathered whom.

"The Angus knows which bloodlines may cross and which must go their separate ways," Thea's grandmother said, "and it's best to leave love out of it." Thea thought it wasn't too different from how she bred the dogs, though she wasn't about to say that to Rowen.

Yet things were not always so simple—Lana had visited the Angus for years, but never had a baby. Her aunt didn't talk about it anymore, but Thea knew that she hadn't entirely given up—she still pounded her special herbs every night and drank them down in hot water before bed.

The children in the main house now stood shifting their weight from leg to leg, casting their eyes about the house and wondering, she knew, where the pups might be hiding themselves.

She and Dolan led them onto the sands where their companions, ten days old, huddled against their mother. The big Chikchu looked up at Thea comfortably; this was her fourth litter, and she knew that her pups would be returned before long.

One at a time, Thea solemnly introduced the children to their Chikchu pups, intoning, "I give you Phoenix, your one companion," "I give you Ursa, your one companion," as she handed each animal to reaching hands. All of the Chikchu were named after heavenly bodies; her Peg's full name was Pegasus. Perry ruined his introduction by smiling rudely up at Thea and asking, "But some have *two* companions, isn't that right?" Thea glared at him and moved on to the next child.

It was true that she had two companions. Her mother's Chikchu had refused to leave Thea's side after Mai's death. Lana said it was a great relief to everyone that Gru didn't choose to starve herself to death, as some Chikchu did after losing their human companions. Thea and Gru were said to have been quite a sight, the not-yet-walking baby dwarfed by the huge gray dog. Thea could still remember clutching handfuls of Gru's fur as she learned to walk, and then skate. But Gru was never playful. Thea

58

often felt that she had one companion, Peg, and two aunts: Lana and Gru.

Showing the children how to properly hold their tiny pups, she led the newly joined pairs to sit in a group on the sand. Then Thea spoke about the history of the Chikchu as faithful companions to their people, first in the cold world above and then, after settlement, in Gracehope. She never said anything too important during the first assembly. She knew that the children couldn't really pay attention in the excitement of first seeing their companions, who were now scrambling around comically on the sands.

Thea watched sympathetically as the children reluctantly returned the pups to their mother. She reminded the group of their visiting privileges and then gently propelled them back toward the main house. In a few weeks they would take their companions home with them, bound for life.

Perry was so besotted with his little black-and-white pup that Thea had to shove him along. Perhaps there was hope for him after all. After lavishing praise and thanks upon pups and mother, Thea returned to Cassie.

Cassie panted and stood from time to time, turning a tight circle inside the box and then settling down again. Dolan brought over two large lightglobes, each set at half-light.

"It's going quickly," Thea said. "She's ready."

Dolan nodded. "I'll watch this time, if you don't mind."

Thea blinked, not sure whether to believe. "I . . . I'm to birth her?"

"I'll be right here." Dolan settled on the ground. Norma lay down beside him.

There was no time for Thea to feel honored—or fearful. She turned back to Cassie. "All right, let's meet those beautiful strong pups of yours."

The first pup was pure white. Just like Peg, Thea thought, feeling a quick stab of love for her own companion. Cassie raised her head to lick her new daughter clean, and the pup started breathing on her own. She suckled for a few minutes while Cassie rested, but Thea soon moved the newborn into the heated bed that would hold the pups until the whole litter was ready to return to the whelping box.

The next six births went smoothly. By the time Cassie started the breathing of pup number seven, Thea was elated.

"Seven pups! I haven't seen a litter of seven pups in a twelvemonth, have you?"

Dolan shook his head, smiling broadly. Thea allowed herself a long sigh as she helped the last pup find his mother's milk. Then something brought her up short.

The sounds were so faint she hadn't noticed them at first: a faint keening, like a high-pitched hum that stopped and then started again.

"Cassie is signaling!" she said.

Thea had to stay completely motionless to hear the exhausted Chikchu. She closed her eyes and focused on the pattern of sound that emerged, the distinct rising and falling of tone that was perceptible only to ear adepts like herself. Thea was tired, too, and she had to listen through the entire sequence several times before she understood.

Another.

"She's not finished!" Thea cried. Dolan stood up. But despite Thea's best efforts and encouragement, no pup emerged. Thea was sure now that there was another pup. Cassie's eyes fluttered open and closed as she struggled to maintain consciousness.

"She's too tired," Dolan said, hovering but not yet taking control.

Thea unclasped her bracelets, scattering them to the sands and cursing herself for not having done so earlier. She was losing time.

Putting one hand against Cassie's shoulder, she reached into the sticky warmth of the dog with the other. She felt the still body of the last pup and brought it carefully out into the air. Half the size of the others, he lay limp in Thea's hand, not breathing. Dolan silently handed her a clean square of fur and she wiped the tiny dog down with it. Then Thea stretched the pup out across her forearm, stroking its head and back with more pressure. She could feel the animal's heart beating faintly against her wrist as she urged it to live, vaguely aware of Dolan standing perfectly still beside her.

The pup remained motionless for a long moment and then took breath, shuddering. Thea exhaled, realizing that she had stopped breathing herself for a minute, and set the runt quickly to the warmth of his sleeping mother.

Even the unflappable Dolan was awed. Eight live pups and a healthy mother! Thea gathered all the pups around Cassie and positioned the heater at their backs.

"Take another look at the runt, Thea," Dolan said.

"Is something wrong?" She examined the tiny creature again as he sucked contentedly at his mother's milk. He was a pretty one, with a light-gray coat and—Thea checked all four to make sure—yes, white paws!

She sucked in her breath. "Dolan . . ."

Four white paws: The pup bore the legend's mark.

When the Settlers arrived in the cold world, they met a pack of wild dogs, or wolf-dogs, that they named the Chikchu. The Chikchu became the Settlers' guides; the dogs showed them safe places to cross the ice and helped them hunt for skins to wear and food to eat. It was written that Sarah, Grace's granddaughter, was particularly close to her Chikchu, a dark-colored dog with four white paws.

Every Chikchu in Gracehope was descended from those first dogs. Some were black, some all-white, some had dark masks across their eyes, or four dark paws, or three white and one dark, or two of each. But never in anyone's memory was there a Chikchu born with four white paws. Until tonight.

A legend had grown: People said that Sarah's white-footed Chikchu was a symbol of the Settlers' journey to Gracehope, and that another would not be born until it was safe to cross the cold world again. Thea had never believed it.

Dolan gazed at the pup. "He's weak, and small. We'll keep an eye on him before saying anything." He stroked Norma and broke into a smile. "You did wonderfully."

They grinned at each other. When Thea started yawning, Dolan said, "Don't worry about the timelog. You've done more than nine hours' work tonight. Go home."

Thea shook her head. "No favors," she said firmly. "You know I have to be extra careful. Anyway, I'd like to stay until Cassie wakes."

Dolan shrugged. "Suit yourself, girl."

Thea stretched out on the sand, resting her head on the edge of the whelping box, where the pups now slept as soundly as Cassie did. Sometime later, she was dimly aware that Dolan was slipping a fur under her head; Norma's tail swept her arm as they walked away again. Grateful, she slept.

FIVE

PETER

NORTHWEST GREENLAND

I n America, you're always in a place with a name: You're in New York City, or in Orange County, or in the middle of Lake Huron. You are somewhere.

In Greenland, Peter learned, things are different. If you aren't in one of the little towns that dot the coastline, you aren't necessarily in any named place at all. When Peter asked where exactly in Greenland they would be living, his father always said they would be "up on the ice sheet, near a town called Qaanaaq."

From the Air National Guard plane, Qaanaaq was a

little cluster of colored squares next to the ocean. His father shouted to Peter (you had to shout to be heard over the engine) that the squares were small wooden houses made with lumber brought in by boat. There were no trees in Greenland.

Peter's whole body was vibrating with the rattling plane. There were no passenger seats. Instead, they sat back against some thick red netting that was slung from floor to ceiling, anchored by big metal clips. It was also cold. Hours before, Jonas had turned to him and shouted, "Is your butt numb yet?"

"Like ice!" Peter had shouted back.

The plane circled, giving Peter's stomach a lurch, and then started down. He stretched to see what the pilot was aiming for, but there was only flat, white ice below.

"Why do they call it Greenland if it's covered in ice?" Miles had asked him. Peter had no idea.

Now he leaned toward Jonas and yelled the same question.

Jonas smiled and cupped his hands around his mouth to shout. "False advertising!"

When the plane landed, Peter was stiff and cold. One of the pilots grabbed him by the hand and pulled him to his feet. He wished he could stagger into a coffee shop and order a hot chocolate and French fries. He got to the door of the plane and saw nothing but white ground and gray sky. He jumped down next to his mother, who was squinting against the wind and scanning the horizon.

Peter's father hopped down beside him. "Got your gloves? Great. Let's start unloading."

The pilots helped. They worked in silence because the noise of the engine was practically deafening. Peter's father had explained that no one turned an engine off on the ice cap—it was so cold that you might not get it started again.

There were boxes and boxes of stuff, and it felt good to move around again. Dr. Solemn and Jonas showed Peter and his mom how to make a cargo line, which was just a bunch of boxes lined up straight so that you could find them after a snowstorm. The pilots unloaded a few huge flat bundles that Peter's father said would eventually be their tent. There were smaller flat bundles that would be the dogs' shelter. The dogs were coming from Qaanaaq in a few days. It was against the law to bring dogs into Greenland—the Inuit wanted to keep their breeds pure, Jonas said.

The pilots stayed long enough to help set up the two little nylon tents they would live in for the first few days, Peter and Jonas sharing one while his parents took the other. Each tent had to be pinned down by twelve long rods so it wouldn't blow away. When the last bamboo stick had been driven into the snow and the propane stove was declared functional, the pilots shook hands all around, got into their plane, and were gone.

It was blissfully quiet. Peter stood outside his tent looking at the snow that stretched out forever in every direction. His father was rummaging in one of the cargo boxes, looking nothing like Superman. The wind had died.

What in the world would he do here for the next six weeks?

His dad turned around and called, "I've found dinner! Beef stew or chicken pot pie?"

"Stew!"

"Gotcha. And a bag of brownies!"

Things were looking up.

The days that followed were wet and tiring: Peter helped build the new tent, which came with a set of instructions as big as a phone book and a video they had no way of watching. He hauled buckets of snow to melt for water, nailed boards for the dogs' shelter, washed dishes in freezing cold water. The glare of the sun was everywhere.

He didn't sleep well. He was used to honking trucks and car alarms, but the screaming wind was new. And the tent he and Jonas shared was covered in puddles from the snow they tracked in on their boots. Anything that touched the floor got soaking wet.

And then, finally, the new tent was finished. Moving-in day was a celebration complete with steak, cake, and snow peas. Peter's father said a celebration wasn't a celebration without steak and cake. And his mother loved snow peas.

When Peter woke up the next morning, life seemed wonderful. He was in a bed. The floor was dry. The bread-maker had worked and the tent smelled like a bakery. Then, at breakfast, Peter's dad announced that he was taking a dogsled and going to Qaanaaq. But he was bringing Jonas with him, not Peter.

An hour later, Peter frowned into the glare of bright sun on snow as he watched Jonas check the dogs' harnesses while Dr. Solemn gave the sled straps a final tug. "This stinks," he said. He had practically begged to go.

"Don't give me a hard time about this, Pete." Dr. Solemn adjusted his goggles. "I haven't made this trip in years, and I want to make sure it's safe." He yelled over Peter's head toward the tent. "We're off, Rory!"

Jonas knew his way around a dogsled. He'd already given Peter two driving lessons. Peter was great with the harnesses and lines, and he was getting much better at not falling off the sled. But the dogs never listened to him. When Peter said "Cha!" the dogs just stood around nosing in the snow or smelling one another.

"Am I saying it wrong?" Peter had asked. "You said a five-year-old can do this!"

"You've got the sound right," Jonas had said, "but you have to say it like you mean it. Like you expect to actually go somewhere."

Peter's father drove a dogsled as subtly as he parallel-parked their car in the city, and he refused to travel any other way. "Dogs know what's up," he'd told Peter. "When your survival is at stake, they don't give up, and that's more than I can say for any snowmobile."

Now Peter looked bitterly at the eight dogs gathered in front of him. There was a shotgun strapped to the sled in case they met any polar bears as they got closer to the coast, where bears did their hunting. Peter had made his father promise not to shoot one unless absolutely necessary. "Don't worry," his father had said, "nine times out of ten I can scare them off with a few flares." This dad was very different from the city dad who wore corduroys to work and came home with corny jokes and Chinese take-out. This one was serious a lot of the time. And busy.

Peter's mother emerged from the bright blue dome that was their tent. Her hair was clipped up in a bun on top of her head, which meant that she had been writing.

The dogs crowded each other, eager to move.

"You can't take Sasha," Peter said darkly, knowing that they weren't planning to. Sasha was a black-and-white husky, Peter's favorite. She was smarter than the rest of them, and a lot more affectionate.

"Does it look like we're taking her?" His father was getting annoyed.

"Bon voyage," Peter's mother said brightly. "We'll see you in a couple of days." She put an arm around Peter's shoulders as Jonas and Dr. Solemn set off, trotting due west alongside the loaded sled. Then she called after them: "Remember to bring back everything they have that's green!"

The trip to Qaanaaq had two purposes. Peter's father had discovered that the tubing on his steam drill was cracked, and a replacement waited for him at the post office. And they were also going to the town's sole grocery store. Peter's mother said her brain couldn't function without fresh fruit or vegetables.

Their camp was on a small rise on the ice cap, and Peter watched as his father and Jonas quickly descended the side of it and were gone. He held his gaze steady for a few moments, until the fluttering began, just at the edges of his vision. He blinked quickly, banishing it. It had become a game.

Peter shielded his eyes from the sun with a gloved hand. "I'm going to take Sasha for a walk," he told his mother. He knew it was silly to walk a dog in Greenland—they were outside most of the time. But he had always wanted a dog to walk, and this trip seemed like his only chance. Their apartment building didn't allow pets.

"Be careful. Daddy really worries about you, you

know," his mother said. "It's a lot of responsibility, having you here. I think it's a bit scary for him."

"Well, maybe he shouldn't have invited me, then. We could have stayed home, like we always do. Or I could have stayed with Miles." He pictured himself eating oranges and popcorn with Miles on his dad's TV couch. Not so bad.

"Don't be silly."

"Right, no silliness," Peter said as he ducked into the low shed that was the dogs' shelter. Momentarily blinded by the dimness, he called, "Here, girl." Sasha was waiting just inside the door for him. She followed him into the sunlight and flipped onto her back so he could rub her belly.

Peter had been warned over and over that sled dogs weren't pets in Greenland. Here, dogs were fed and tied to stakes outside until needed for travel or to hunt. They were important, and cared for, but they were not part of the family. In town, dogs that managed to get loose from their stakes by slipping their harnesses or gnawing through their leads were seen as a danger to the community, and shot dead on sight.

But Sasha was different. "Someone has been showing this animal a lot of love," Peter's mother said, watching Sasha submit happily to Peter's crazy tickles. "She's somebody's darling, all right."

And she would be somebody's darling again, she

meant. His mother always managed to remind him that this arrangement was temporary. She didn't want him to get too attached. He pushed the thought away. For now, Sasha was his.

Peter squatted next to the dog and scanned the camp. He never got tired of looking at their tent. It was a bright blue dome, pocked all over, so that it looked like a golf ball half-submerged in the ice. He and Jonas called it the "geebee geebee," which stood for "giant blue golf ball."

The inside of the tent was as wonderful as the outside. There were three separate bunk areas, each with drawers under the bed and a small bookshelf built into the headboard. Each bed had a reading light that cast a perfect cone of yellow light at just the right angle. Peter's parents had a double-size bed and two reading lights. There were round windows like portholes all around, curtains to be drawn across the foot of each bed for privacy, and the tiniest bathroom Peter had ever seen.

The kitchen area had two propane burners, a microwave, and the breadmaker (it was Peter's job to measure the ingredients and set the timer every night). There was also a bucket to take outside and fill with snow to boil for water. There was no need for a refrigerator.

In the middle of the tent was a round table and four chairs. Jonas acted all excited about having his very own chair, and taped a joke sign to the back of one. "Jonas's chair."

Outside, three brightly colored ropes, about knee-high, fanned out from the geebee geebee. One led to the research tent, one to the dogs' long, low shelter, and one to the cargo line. Peter's father said they might need something to hold on to in a storm, and he'd made Peter memorize which colored rope led to which place. For now, they were just something to trip over.

"C'mon, girl." Peter stood up and Sasha happily rolled to her feet next to him. He put one hand on her head and gestured to the horizon with the other. "Time to look for the Second Volkswagen Road."

His mother laughed. "Don't believe everything you hear."

The Second Volkswagen Road was something Jonas talked about, a road on the ice cap built in secret by Volkswagen as a private test site for new cars. Jonas said the failures—all never-before-seen prototypes—were abandoned on the ice, and Peter intended to find one.

"It's on the Internet, Mom."

"No, that's the first Volkswagen Road. The *only* Volkswagen Road. And it's a hundred miles south of here."

"That's the test site they *talk* about, Mom. But Jonas read about a second road, where the super-secret models are driven, the stuff that really breaks new ground. No one is supposed to know where it is, because the car companies spy on each other with flyovers and satellites."

"Ah." Mrs. Solemn released her hair and it dropped in

73

dark waves around the shoulders of her jacket. "So this road could be anywhere, I suppose."

"It *could* be anywhere. But I can't look anywhere, can I? It could be *dangerous*. My boots might get dirty. So I guess I'll just look around here."

His mother rolled her eyes. "Poor thing. Your parents never take you anywhere exciting like the arctic circle. Well, good luck. Be back before lunch. Check your watch."

Peter decided to head east. The ground sloped gradually away from camp, and he slid along happily next to Sasha in his boots. She never strained at her leash, but trotted next to him, apparently as interested in finding the road as he was.

Twenty minutes later, Peter's nose and cheeks were half-numb with cold and he was ready to turn around. So much for his big walk, he thought, starting back to camp. He looked steadily up at the geebee geebee as he walked, knowing that he was waiting for the fluttering to start. He knew that he shouldn't let it, that it would bring on one of his headaches and he would have to spend the rest of the morning in bed. But something compelled him.

After a minute, there was a faint pulsing. The tent was animated as if by a tiny heart, beating fast. He knew he should look away now. Blink, he told himself.

And then the geebee geebee loomed in front of him as

if he had put a pair of binoculars to his eyes. He could see the weave of the blue fabric. He noticed that the door flaps hadn't been closed all the way—the zipper pull hung a few inches from the top. He was seeing it more clearly than he had when he stood three feet in front of it with his mother.

Sasha barked once, and his gaze jerked at the sound, causing an uncomfortable moment of darkness before his sight returned to normal and he saw her a few paces away. He had dropped her leash. "I'm coming," he said. Five steps later, he felt the headache break over him like a wave.

When he walked into the tent, carefully zipping the first set of door flaps closed before opening the inner flaps, his mother was at the table with her hair in its bun. She was doodling on a pad, lots of words and arrows pointing from one to another.

"Find any Lamborghinis?" she asked. A bowl of tuna salad sat on the table.

"There's always tomorrow," Peter said, heading straight to his bunk.

"Aren't you hungry?"

"More tired," he said. His head held a tiny raging storm. "I'll eat later, okay?"

After an hour or so, he could sit up. His mother was still in her chair. Her pad, full of circles and arrows and scientific nonsense syllables, was pushed to one side, and she was writing in a notebook with a red cover he hadn't seen before. Her hand moved across the page so quickly he wondered that she had time to think of the words. He watched her for a few minutes before she glanced up and saw him.

She flipped the book closed and gave him a strained smile. "Hungry yet?"

He was.

SIX

THEA

"All this fuss for seven people." Thea lifted a large serving platter and frowned at the crowded table. "I don't think we can fit in one more thing. It's impossible."

"Hush, Thea." Lana crossed the greatroom, the hem of her heavy robe sweeping the floor as she moved across it. It was one of Thea's favorites, the embroidery all in yellow, with a squared neckline and a blue sash that tied in back. Though worn, the robe was still quite elegant. And only Lana could fashion a rose from the loose ends of a thick sash with her hands behind her back.

Thea's aunt took the platter, which was glazed a bright amber with a design of dark red leaves, and began shifting dishes around the cluttered tabletop.

"I'll finish this. You should change."

Thea looked down at the fur she wore. "Change? Why? I put this on when I got home this morning."

"I'm not going to answer that. Please be sure that it's a robe without stains."

Thea started to argue, but turned and went off, determined not to take her feelings out on Lana. She had come home from the breeding grounds at first light, elated and ravenous. Her aunt glowed as Thea told her about Cassie's litter. Then Thea had tried to rest, her thoughts straying to Rowen before she finally dozed off. She woke in a sour mood.

Thea opened her trunk and took out three folded robes. Her favorite, the violet, was still stained despite her aunt's repeated reminders to clean it. A blue one had a frayed hem. The last robe Lana had embroidered with broad colorful flowers: Thea had always loved it. But tonight the robe looked childish to her.

At the bottom of Thea's trunk rested a few of her mother's robes. When she was little, Thea had tried them on from time to time, trailing them on the floor while Lana admired her as she circled the greatroom. Now one of them caught her eye, an ivory robe with an intricate pattern of winding vines in pale green.

78

Thea lifted it to her shoulders. She threw off her fur and slipped into the robe, cinching it tightly around her waist with a bright-red sash.

When Thea stepped into the greatroom, Lana gazed at her for a long moment. "A good thing you thought of it," her aunt said briskly. She piled slices of bread into a basket. "In another twelvemonth that will be short in the arm."

"Can you help me with this?" Thea held out her mother's bone locket, suspended by a length of red ribbon. Lana crossed to her and took the ends of the ribbon carefully, then gestured for Thea to turn and hold up her hair.

When the locket was settled at her throat, Thea felt she could face the evening in front of her. She smiled at her aunt. "What can I do to help?"

Lana smiled back. "Turn around again so that I can sash you properly."

She had just finished when everyone began to arrive, Sela, Ezra, and Mattias coming in through the dock door just as Thea's grandmother, Rowen, called from the Mainway entrance.

"Help!" Sela cried, staggering in from her sleigh with a lidded basket. She flushed at the sight of Thea in Mai's robe, but her voice was light. "That's a sevennight's fruit rations. Losh, it's heavy."

Thea took the load and settled it on the basin counter. Mattias came through the door with two more bundles.

"Those are for you, Thea," Sela said. "The furs I spoke of yesterday."

Thea took them from Mattias and started toward her bedchamber. "You shouldn't have, Sela. But thank you."

She left the furs in a heap on her bed and returned to the greatroom, where Lana cast her a meaningful look.

Thea sighed. There was no way to avoid her grandmother without looking childish. She lifted two of the tall drinks from Lana's tray and crossed the room to where Rowen and Sela stood together.

Rowen smiled as she accepted her glass and then beckoned Thea closer and fingered the embroidery on her robe. "I would swear upon my line that this is my work. I remember your mother wearing it. But she was no younger than ten and six. It couldn't be the same robe."

Lana stepped up next to Thea. "I was surprised myself to see her in it. The embroidery is beautifully preserved, don't you think, Mother? Your work always lasts. And it suits her so."

"Indeed it does," Rowen said thoughtfully. "And is that your mother's locket, Thea? I haven't seen it in a dozen years. Are the portraits still inside? I would like to see them again."

No one spoke as Thea opened the locket and held it up between finger and thumb. Rowen peered down at the pictures. "Very nice. Thea! *Look* at those fingernails."

Thea let the locket fall and curled her fingers into her

palms. She chewed her nails, particularly when her lump of ambergris was not at hand, and her grandmother always gave her trouble about it.

Lana changed the subject. "I've two new dyes I'm working on, a deep orange-red and a bright purple. I had hoped to have the fine opinions of our chief weaver and master artist," she said as she steered Rowen and Sela toward her worktable.

Thea found Mattias stacking the fruit from his mother's basket.

"Let's go settle the dogs," he said. "I have to give Ham some water."

"Mattias! Don't you know enough to water your dogs before coming in? The poor things are probably desperate."

The Chikchu were resting comfortably next to Sela's docked sleigh. Thea greeted the dogs and gave each of them a long drink from the dock pump before freeing them from their sleigh traces.

"Let's take them in to the others," she said to Mattias. "I know Peg would love to see Ham. They can visit until you go home."

"Is it safe?" he asked, a little embarrassed. "What if Peg is nearing her . . . her time?" Unlike Cassie and the rest of her littermates, Peg had not yet mated.

Thea laughed as she ducked into the low companion chamber next to the sled dock. "She's not ready. I would know, Mattias."

Ham and Peg were indeed happy to see each other, frolicking briefly until they woke the older dogs, including Lana's companion, Aries, and Rowen's Lynx. Many Chikchu lived as long as their human companions, but the oldest dogs slept through most of their last years.

Ham dug himself a depression in the sand next to Peg's well-worn bed. There was something solid and protective about Ham that reminded Thea of Mattias.

"He's not signaling to you, is he?" Mattias asked anxiously.

"No," Thea said, smiling at her cousin. "I was just thinking how well he looks."

"Good," said Mattias. He was a generous soul, but Thea knew he wasn't happy that she could hear Ham's signals when he could not. She'd explained a hundred times that Chikchu didn't signal often, and that when they did it was usually only a word or two. But Mattias still seemed to imagine that she and Ham gossiped regularly in secret.

When they returned to the greatroom, the family was seated at the table, and Thea and Mattias separated. They were forbidden to sit together at these events. Rowen disliked what she called their "private exchanges."

When all were settled, Rowen raised her glass. Her fingernails were perfect.

The first-line suppers always began with the same three words. Thea despised them.

"To Thea's daughters," Rowen said gravely.

Thea stared at her plate. She could never make it through one of these evenings without being reminded that the survival of the first bloodline now depended on her. What if she had sons, like Sela? What if she couldn't have children at all, like Lana? Or what if she didn't *want* to have children, like Peg?

Everyone but Thea responded—"Thea's daughters"—and they began to eat.

"And happy birthday to me!" Ezra shouted.

Thea grinned. "Yes," she said. "Happy birthday to Ezra!"

The dock door burst open. "Sorry to be late again," Dolan said, taking the seat next to his sister, Sela. "A messenger arrived just as I was leaving, and I had to make a call."

"What was it?" Thea asked.

Dolan was loading his plate with food. "A stone wedged in a forepaw. Easy enough to fix."

Sela passed her brother the bread. "You'll be able to send Thea on those errands soon."

But Dolan acted as if he hadn't heard. "Thea, have you given any thought to names for Cassie's pups?"

Thea flushed happily. She hadn't been sure she would be allowed to name them.

"Libra, Fornax, Pyxis, Polaris, Io, Europa, Ganymede, and Callisto." The names tumbled out on top of one another in a single breath.

Dolan burst out laughing, setting off the others as well.

"Well, it seems you have given the subject a bit of thought," Dolan said when things had quieted.

"Dolan!" Sela interrupted. "You've just reminded me. Why ever didn't you tell us about the pup bearing the legend's mark? Is it true? The legend pup! Birthed by my own line, and I hear of it through ninth-line gossip!"

Thea thought she saw Rowen stiffen, and she wondered whether her grandmother had heard as well. Thea herself had told no one but Mattias, early that morning on her way home, and she was sure that he hadn't breathed a word of it.

Dolan scowled. "It's just a child's story, Sela." He glanced at Ezra, who was busy rolling a pea around the edge of his plate.

"Not to some it isn't," Sela said.

Dolan swallowed. "He's a runt, born small and slow to breathe. Thea and I agreed that it might be better not to speak of him yet, just in case. In fact, I'd like to know how word of it got out. . . ."

"It wasn't Thea," Mattias said quickly.

"No, I hadn't suspected Thea," Dolan said with an amused look. "It was probably one of the messengers, though I've no doubt *you* knew about the pup, Mattias."

Mattias was suddenly preoccupied with his napkin. Thea looked guiltily at her lap.

"So I *am* the last to know!" Sela said, throwing up her hands.

Thea's grandmother patted Sela's shoulder. "Hardly, my dear. Hardly the last."

When everyone had eaten, Lana stood up and began to clear the long table, nodding to Thea that it was time to ready the fruit. Mattias joined her at the counter and helped her cut the heavy rounds into wedges.

"That was about as much fun as usual," he murmured. Thea grinned at him.

Lana brought them a small candle for Ezra's plate. "And remember to set some fruit aside for your grandmother, Mattias," she said quietly.

Mattias's grandmother Dexna was Rowen's older sister, and a respected healer. But Dexna couldn't speak: not a word. She rarely joined the first-line suppers, and Thea saw her only when she visited Rowen, who lived with Dexna next door. Dexna was invariably reading in the greatroom, her silver hair tied in a thick shining knot. Dexna disliked lightslates, and insisted upon reading bound paper books from the ancient collection that sat in the archive, a borrowing privilege bestowed upon her alone, as far as Thea knew.

She passed Mattias a bowl and watched him fill it with sweet orange fruit.

*   *   *

When the guests had gone, Lana waved away Thea's offers to clean. "Sela and Mattias helped. And you didn't have any real sleep last night."

Thea didn't argue. She longed to get out of her robe and its tight sash. She began to unclasp her bracelets as she crossed the greatroom.

Sela's furs lay piled on her bed: nestled on top of them was a paper scroll tied with a bright red ribbon.

Thea stared at it. Then she lifted it gently and slipped off the ribbon. The tightly rolled paper jumped to life in her hand. She unrolled it, afraid at first that the paper would crack. But the document was not as old as it appeared: It unfurled quickly, almost without a sound.

It was a map.

SEVEN

PETER

Peter's parents reminded him of things: He wasn't to start the cooking stove. There were snacks on the counter. He shouldn't touch the heating stove. The dogs shouldn't need anything, so there would be no need to cross the camp.

"Why don't you just say 'stay inside the tent' and be done with it?" Peter murmured.

"Don't exaggerate," his father said. "You are perfectly free to leave the tent. But every one of these things is a matter of survival, Peter." He shouldered a heavy pack jammed with equipment for the afternoon's fieldwork.

No gun, this time—they were headed east, away from the coast and the bears.

"Are you sure you don't want to come with us?" Peter's mother was stuffing a plastic bag of dried fruit into her already bulging backpack. He was relieved that she was going. She'd been hunched over her red notebook for nearly the whole time his father and Jonas had been away in Qaanaaq, writing and writing with a glazed look on her face. Sometimes he'd had to call her three or four times before she looked up.

"No thanks," Peter said. "I'm still numb from yesterday. I'm going to read in bed under all of my covers." He also intended to finish off the pan of brownies left over from lunch.

Peter's father and Jonas had come back from Qaanaaq with new tubing for the steam drill and a lot of onions and carrots, which was all there was at the grocery store in town ("I guess we can make stir-fry," Peter's mother had said sadly). Then the four of them had set out with a dogsled to make fieldwork rounds together. The sledding was wonderful. They swept across the ice in the sunlight, the dogs barking with joy.

But then they stopped to work. It had been freezing, and the fieldwork itself was not very interesting: His father adjusted his equipment and mumbled things to himself, Jonas dug a deep hole and wrote numbers down in a notebook, and there was a lot of staring at little pins stuck into the ice. His mother spent the whole time scanning the horizon with a pair of binoculars. She said she was looking for musk oxen or arctic fox. Peter saw his father raise his eyebrows at her a couple of times, but she just shook her head and said, "Nothing." Meanwhile, Peter jogged in circles to keep warm.

He'd be just fine staying alone at camp today.

Jonas popped his head into the tent through the door flaps, his cheeks deep pink with cold. "Sled's all set." Dr. Solemn passed him the last two packs before turning back to Peter.

"We'll be gone about four hours. Satellite weather says it'll remain fair, but winds come up quickly here. Just maintaining the camp for a few hours is a big responsibility, Peter."

"Right. Don't worry, Dad."

Three hours later, Peter was wishing he had asked a few more questions. It had been snowing for two hours. There was at least three feet of fresh snow on the ground, and the storm showed no sign of letting up. So much for the satellite weather service.

His parents were safe, he told himself. His father had probably been in fifty storms as bad as this one, and they always took all of their bad-weather equipment with them, just in case. They must be waiting out the storm somewhere, holed up in their hard-weather pods. At least he hoped they were.

He knew he would be fine inside the geebee geebee, but what about Sasha and the other dogs his parents had left behind? Their little shed was low, and it had a flat roof. What if they were buried? Or worse, what if the thing collapsed under the weight of the snow that was piling up on it? They could be suffocating already! Why hadn't he taken them into the geebee geebee as soon as the storm started?

There was nothing but whipping snow to be seen through the window next to his bed. He imagined Sasha and the other dogs trapped in the airless shed, or crushed beneath its roof.

He threw his covers back and stood up. He'd wasted a whole hour staring at the blue ceiling and waiting for his parents to come back. His heart beat quickly as he pulled on his warmest jacket and took a long storm rod from the gearbox. His father had told him never to go out in even the lightest snow without one. If things got windy, he was to jab the sharp end into the ground as hard as he could and hang on until the gust passed. It sounded good in theory. Now he wished he'd had a little practice.

He zipped the tent's inner door closed behind him and stood in the tiny space between the geebee geebee's two sets of door flaps. The family had dubbed it "the lobby." At his feet were the colored ropes that led to the camp's other buildings.

He bent down and grabbed hold of the blue line, the

other end of which, he fervently hoped, was secured to the wall of the dogs' shed. Peter unzipped the outer door flaps and stopped.

The wind was moaning, with a little high-pitched scream thrown in every few seconds. He stayed just inside the doorway, listening and watching the heavy snow jump every which way. Then, feeling like he was stepping off the end of the earth, he pushed out into the storm, holding on to the blue rope with one gloved hand while he jerked the tent's zipper closed with the other.

One step from the tent, Peter was blind and deaf with snow. And very cold. His first instinct was to turn back.

He doubled over to hold on to the rope, lifting it out of the snow with effort as he went. He made slow progress, counting his paces. Every one of them was hard won. Half his energy was spent trying to pry the blue rope from the deep snow so that he could keep his grip on it. The little bits of him directly exposed to the elements— the skin around his eyes and mouth that his mask didn't completely cover—felt as if they were being lightly pricked by a thousand small needles. No, a thousand icicles.

After step nineteen, he convinced himself that it would be easier to let go of the rope and make a run for it, now that he knew which direction to go. He'd dressed in a hurry, and the snow had found its way into his clothes— down one boot, inside his gloves, up both sleeves, and somehow down his back. His legs throbbed from walking in a crouch. But just as he began to straighten up, a screaming gust of wind burned his face and threatened to blow him across camp. Right. No letting go of the rope.

Twenty-eight. Twenty-nine. On thirty, his right foot seemed to sink a little deeper into the snow than it had on step twenty-nine. And when it came up again, his boot didn't come with it. Peter was balancing on one leg in the middle of an arctic blizzard, looking at his sock. There was no sign of the boot. Holding the blue rope with one hand, he began to plunge his arm into the snow. After five or six tries, he got lucky. The boot had a fair amount of snow in it now, but he jammed his foot right in on top of it.

By the time he got to step number fifty, his progress had become truly painful. On step eighty-two, his face hit the door of the dog's shed.

The snow had drifted up against the small building and the door was covered nearly to Peter's shoulder. It opened in, he remembered gratefully. His father always saw to that kind of detail. He felt for the simple latch and fell into the small shelter on a heap of snow, pushing the door closed behind him and leaning against it for a few moments. If he had had an ounce of energy left, Peter would have started to cry. The room was completely black, its few plastic windows blocked by snow.

He had not thought to bring a flashlight. And his right foot was very cold, and wet.

A short bark—from Sasha?—gave him a sense of where the dogs were huddled together. He could hear them moving around a little, restless and uncertain. He stood, stooping because the ceiling wasn't high enough for him to stand up straight, and felt on the hook by the door for the harness. Six loops. He hoped Jonas and his parents hadn't left more than six dogs. He took off his thick gloves and tucked them carefully into his pockets. If he dropped one, he might never find it again in here.

He knew Sasha would cooperate, but he wasn't so sure about the others. He began to talk in a low voice, feeling his way toward the animals.

Another short bark, close now. He was sure it was Sasha. "Good girl," he told her. "Tell them it's okay."

He felt fur, caught her collar, and rotated it to find the loop. He was surprised by how easily he could arrange the several harness straps properly in the darkness, threading them into their positions almost without thinking. In less than a minute, Sasha was securely harnessed into the lead position. Good. That was one.

After a great deal of groping and a few tangled loops, Peter had the team together. Six dogs. He stuffed his hands back into his gloves, found the door, and opened it. His plan was to loop one end of the harness around the blue rope and give the dogs the command to run.

Sasha was the lead. He could only hope that the others would follow her. He opened the door, noticing with relief that he could see the outlines of the geebee geebee now. It looked far away and ghostly, but at least he could see it. He bent down to find the blue rope in the snow, and knotted the dogs' harness strap to it. Then, summoning his best, most self-confident command voice, he shouted into the still-howling wind.

The dogs were more than ready to run for him. They ran with all of their might. Breaking the blue rope.

Peter was dragged along behind them, shouting "Wrong way, wrong way!" But most of his shouting was muffled by the snow that was being driven into his mouth as he bounced behind the pack. The dogs seemed to draw strength from the storm. Peter clung to the harness strap with two hands, sliding along on the back of his coat as they ran and ran. And ran. And then, miraculously, stopped.

Peter sat up. It took him a few moments to realize that, although a great deal of snow had been driven inside the front of his jacket, he was unhurt. If it weren't for the vicious cold he might have wanted to do it again.

The dogs had stopped because they had come to a nearly vertical wall of ice that rose abruptly out of the snow like a billboard by the side of a highway. Gratefully, he looked up and down the thing before making his way to one edge and peering around to the other side.

Then he was even more grateful. The ground fell away steeply below him, though just how far down it went he couldn't see in the blowing snow. Peter gave a low whistle that made the dogs turn to him expectantly.

They were seated in two neat rows, looking at him as if he would know what to do next. He looked back toward what he thought might be the direction of his family's camp and saw nothing but blowing snow. The wind was rapidly covering their tracks. He had to get the team going again before the trail disappeared completely, but couldn't resist his urge to rest first. Just for a minute.

The ice wall offered some protection from the wind. Sasha dug herself a shallow niche in the snow and sat down with her back against the wall. Thirsty from her long sprint, she started to eat mouthful after mouthful of snow. Peter made his way to the dog and bent to rub her head. He leaned against the wide wall and gazed at a hundred and eighty degrees of white.

He knew they had to start back. Peter forced himself to his feet, bending to brush off the snow that clung to his legs.

Something caught his eye as he was tightening the cords on his boots. There was an object embedded in the ice wall, at about the height of his waist. Something colorful. He squatted down in front of it.

Just beneath the surface of the ice was a ring of bright red. It was sort of woven-looking, or twisted, he thought, looking more closely. And although the glacier was covered with a fine dusting of snow, he realized he was seeing the ring through a patch of clear ice. It was almost as if the thing were behind glass.

He hovered beside the red ring for almost a minute, wondering what it could be. Another of his father's arctic effects? Some kind of sunspot seen by boys who stumbled around for too long in the cold?

He pulled off one glove and put his hand up to the ice that encased the ring—it was as smooth as polished marble, nothing like the rough crystalline stuff that covered the rest of the glacier. He peered hard at the ring beneath it. Maybe it was part of a Volkswagen.

Peter was unaware at first of the fluttering that had begun just at the edge of his vision. It was almost impossible to detect with the snow that still blew all around him. A rushing in his head gave him a moment's warning that something was about to happen, although by then it was too late to stop it.

In an instant the world went from white to red. There was only the color red, eclipsing everything that he knew was around him: the ground under his feet, the dogs beside him, the snow that was everywhere. He felt the wind against his face, but that was all. He blinked furiously, but still saw nothing but red. He was blind. His muscles began to twang with panic, like strings that someone was plucking hard. He held his eyes closed for a few moments, took a deep breath, and opened them again to find that he still couldn't see. The color red was like a blanket over his head, without shape or depth. His whole body began to sing with fear.

Then he became aware of something else: a sharp pain in his hand. He closed his eyes again and thought about the pain, not about the fact that he was blind and lost in a snowstorm on the Greenland ice cap. His hand throbbed. He forced his mind to fall in with the rhythm of it, trying to disengage his eyes from the red ring, willing them to let go of what they had seized.

When he opened his eyes, he was back in the snow with the dogs, who were looking up at him again as if he would know what to do next.

He had left his bare hand resting against the glacier wall, and it was cold. Painfully cold. He snatched it back, stuffing the numb and lifeless thing into his glove as quickly as he could. Its painful throbbing intensified, and now his head joined in.

But he could see. He took a deep breath. Prioritize, he told himself. The snow had let up some. The most important thing now was to get back to camp before he froze to death. Ignoring the headache that was beginning to rage, he steered the dogs to their vanishing trail, called out the command to move, and began running along behind them the best he could.

Sasha picked up the scent of camp just as the tracks

disappeared completely. When it came into view, the strange domes looked like home for the first time. He was relieved enough to want to cry, but too tired.

He practically crawled through the tent flaps, dragging the dogs in after him but leaving them harnessed. Nobody home. Where were his parents and Jonas? He fell into bed and closed his eyes, which muted his headache mercifully. A minute later he was asleep in his coat and boots.

"And somebody's been sleeping in *my* bed!" A voice squeaked near Peter's ear. "And there he is!"

Peter opened his eyes. The headache was gone. And Jonas's face was grinning down at him.

"Goldilocks and the three bears," Jonas said. "Get it?"

"Right," said Peter, not getting it at all. Sitting up, he realized two things.

One, he was in Jonas's bed. Goldilocks. *Now* he got it.

Two, his hand felt like it was on fire.

He was taking his gloves off—the left one very carefully—when his parents came in, stomping the snow off their boots and looking surprised to see the dogs in the tent.

Peter could barely stay awake during dinner. His mother gasped in a satisfying way when he explained how the rope had broken, and shook her head sternly at his father when Dr. Solemn started to say that the dogs would have been fine in the shed without his rescue mission.

"It was very brave of you, Peter," his dad finished quickly. "Really selfless."

Peter's mother was rubbing his hand. He had told her that he took his glove off to untangle a harness line, and then couldn't find it for a while in the snow.

"But you should know that you were also very, very lucky," his father said, "and if you ever go out alone into a storm again, you'll be on the next plane out of here."

Jonas raised one finger. "Excuse me, but when *is* the next plane out of here?"

Dr. Solemn pretended to glare at him.

"Don't worry," Peter said to his father. "Rushing out into the next arctic storm isn't exactly a great temptation."

His parents and Jonas had spent the afternoon awkwardly curled up in their hard-weather pods. Peter thought of Miles pretending to be trapped inside one of them back in their living room in New York. Miles was probably swimming right now, he thought, or he was "rowing crew" in a sweaty T-shirt—either possibility was unreal. Or maybe it was Greenland that was unreal.

Jonas made everyone laugh while they cleaned up after dinner by demonstrating how he'd spent a good part of the afternoon inside his pod trying to get a granola bar out of his pack, poking himself in the eye and getting a terrible cramp in his leg.

When he had drawn his curtain that night, Peter found his little notebook in one of the drawers under the bed. He flipped to the inside cover, made his slash—the number didn't seem important anymore—and, next to it, a star, and, after a moment, another star. Because this time had been different: For the first time since the visions began, today he had felt a tiny measure of control. He had discovered a new muscle. A weak muscle. A muscle he intended to study before he told anyone about it.

EIGHT

THEA

There is something very good about work when your mind is in a state of confusion, Thea thought, mucking manure out of the Chikchu stalls. It was not a job she normally looked forward to.

For the hundredth time she asked herself: Why? Why would someone go to the trouble of finding paper and ink? Why would someone bother to copy an old map that anyone could see hanging at the Main Hall? And then leave it for her without a word?

She recognized the map the instant she saw it. It was

one of the earliest maps of Gracehope, an exact replica of the original that hung in the Exhibition Hall. It showed the lake, the waterwheel, the homes of the old quarter, and just the beginnings of the gardens and crop-growth grounds. Even the Settlers' migration tunnel was sketched in, though it must have been reclaimed by the ice long before the original map was drawn. In flowing letters near the top of the paper were two words: *Grace's Hope,* the original name of the settlement. Over the years, the name of the place had become Gracehope. Pure laziness, Rowen said.

In an upper corner of the map was a sun symbol, and in a lower corner there was a tree-sign signature, which meant that it was drawn by a member of the first bloodline. But it all added up to nothing.

She tied up the sacks of manure. They would be delivered to the gardens later in the afternoon. She washed her hands and went to check on Cassie and her pups.

Almost a week old now, the runt was doing well. He fed even more than the others, fending off his littermates with a tiny white paw if one of them threatened to dislodge him from his milk. Thea smiled as Io tolerated a push in the face from her smallest brother.

"He needs it more than you do," Thea told Io, rubbing her behind the ears. "Don't worry, your mother won't let you starve."

Dolan was coming across the grounds with Norma and

Leda, one of the infirmary dogs. Leda's leg had been broken, but she walked well now.

"If you've finished here, I'd like your help," Dolan said, gesturing to Leda. "I'm going to run her today."

"Of course." Thea stroked the dog while Dolan smoothed a long stretch of sand by dragging a length of cloth on the ground behind him. He had to go over several sections a second time after Norma walked over them. Then he took up a position on the far side of the smoothed sands, Norma next to him.

At his signal, Thea gave Leda the command to run. The Chikchu streaked to Dolan and sat down calmly next to Norma. She certainly looked healthy. Dolan leaned in close to the dog and spread his fingers in a sign that sent her trotting obediently back to the main house. Thea found her ambergris in a pocket and kneaded it with one hand as she walked slowly toward Dolan, her head bent to inspect Leda's tracks.

"Well?" asked Dolan, walking to meet her.

"Her gait looks healthy enough," Thea began, "good reach with the forelegs as she starts off. And the tracks move into a single file here as she gathers speed." She pointed to where the prints converged from two lines to one.

"Good. Anything else?"

Thea looked more carefully. "I think she's still favoring it, not at the trot, but at the run."

"What tells you that?"

"Down there, the prints are equally deep." Thea pointed back toward where the dog had begun to gather speed. "But here, where she's running hard and the prints are single file, some are deeper than others." With one hand, she indicated a light paw print, clearly imprinted on the sand, but too shallow to have borne much weight.

"So . . ."

"So, under stress, the leg still hurts her. She needs more rest. A little time in the lake, perhaps." All of the Chikchu loved to swim, and there was no better regimen for mending bones.

"Nicely done." Dolan straightened, smiling broadly. "Pronounce her well now, and you risk lasting damage."

Thea smiled at his praise, but her mind was on the map.

"A favor, Dolan?" It seemed a good time to ask.

Dolan feigned shock. "A favor? I understood that you don't ask for favors."

"Only when I absolutely must," Thea said earnestly. "I know I'm to work this afternoon, but I have a research essay that was to be ready at the end of last term." She hated to lie, but she couldn't wait any longer.

"Scrambling a little these days, Thea?" Dolan was smiling again. "Your aunt thinks you're stretched a bit thin."

Thea smiled. "Then I'm afraid I have two favors to ask."

Dolan waved her off. "Go. And I won't mention anything to Lana. Though if you give me any real reason to worry, I won't hold my tongue. And I'll see you here at first light tomorrow."

Thea went to collect her skates, stopping to check on Cassie's pups. Io was finally getting her fill, while the runt slept, tucked under his mother's chin.

The Mainway was busy. Thea stayed to the right, among the faster skaters, and before long she was at the archive.

Gracehope's archive housed the old books and records. Everything that had happened since the first year of settlement was recorded somewhere in those rooms: births, council-meeting minutes, crop reports, even the Chikchu family trees. Only siring records were kept separately, under the protection of the Angus.

When Thea walked in, the archivist, Lucian, was at his worktable, head bent to an open book. He was alone.

"Good afternoon, Lucian," Thea said. "I have a question, if you can spare a few moments."

"Doubtless you actually have two or more questions." Lucian's head stayed bowed, one dark lock of hair hanging into his face.

Although Lucian was only about Lana's age, something

about his constant seething made him seem older. He was square-jawed, with lots of lines around his eyes, probably from squinting at old texts, and he never looked a person in the eye.

"I'm wondering about the early maps, from the Settlement era."

Lucian turned a page. "That is not a question."

Thea flushed. "Yes, well, I'm wondering if there's any way to know who drew them. One in particular. I know the artist was of the first line, but I don't know exactly . . ."

Lucian looked up, suspicious.

"You know the artist is of the first line, do you? How?"

"In a—in a corner, the right-hand lower corner, just the one map I am thinking of, is the first-line seal, the tree-sign, I mean."

"I know the map you speak of," he said sharply. "Continue."

She took a deep breath. "I was taught that the seal was a form of signature. I wondered if there was any way to find out who . . ."

She stopped, because Lucian was red in the face. He looked as if he might reach out and strangle her. She took a step away. He leaned back in his chair, crossed his arms, and exhaled.

"You were taught that the tree-sign on that map was a form of signature?" He sounded almost friendly.

"Yes."

"And that teaching constituted part of your primary studies."

"Yes."

"And who is your primary tutor?"

"Meriwether."

"Meriwether!" he roared. "That such a man is permitted to instruct others is an affront to our civilization. Just finished with his primaries himself, and none too able a student at that. And now he is muddling the minds of others." He waved her to the worn stone bench in front of his table. She sat.

"The tree-sign on that map is not a form of signature," he said. "We can be sure of this for a simple reason. When that map was drawn, there was no first line."

"No first—"

Lucian held up one finger. "Do not speak until I have finished."

His expression remained stormy. "The tree-sign shows an oak—a tree native to the old world. You are familiar with those along the lakefront."

Thea nodded.

"When our people were hunted and forced to flee the old world, they adopted the image of the tree as a symbol. The tree-sign stood for our people as a whole, and also as a sign of their defiance in the face of the brutality that came close to extinguishing them. It was a symbol of their survival.

"During the years of pursuit, the tree-sign often appeared at a site of slaughter, crudely etched into a nearby tree trunk or scratched out on a stone by someone who had eluded the hunters. The sign was used as a trailmark, to show other survivors the path taken. The symbol has a literal translation from this period: 'One survives.'

"As you know, many of our people died trying to escape the old world, and others were lost in the cold world during the long years that saw the creation of Gracehope. At times it seemed no one would survive to settle it.

"When Grace's granddaughter Sarah gave birth to the settlement's first child"—Lucian nodded briefly at Thea's bracelets—"it was a joyful occasion. The birth of Sarah's daughter was seen as a great victory, a promise that the Settlers could at long last build their civilization in peace. And the sign of the tree, a symbol of survival, became the sign of her bloodline."

Thea nodded. "I—"

Lucian held up a finger. "I haven't yet answered your question. The map you speak of was drawn before the birth of Sarah's daughter. The sign of the tree was not yet associated with the first line, as no such bloodline had been established. The symbol appears on only one map from the Settlement era, and it has always been interpreted to mean, roughly, 'survival.' A logical guess, as the map shows the settlement that represented our people's hope for survival."

Finished, Lucian looked down into his book again.

So there was no first-line mapmaker. Why had the map been left for her?

She stood awkwardly, thanking Lucian with a quick half-bow. Then, though the better part of her brain warned against it, she said, "Why do *you* think there's a tree-sign on that map?"

Lucian blinked and seemed to take an appraising look at Thea, if not an approving one. After a moment he said slowly, " 'Survival' is a close-enough translation. The map's traditional interpretation is much more fundamentally flawed, though it is nothing I am prepared to share at the moment. Don't worry, if you write up a quarter of what I've said, Meriwether is sure to be impressed. It shouldn't take much," Lucian snorted as he looked down again.

She would have to be satisfied with that. Thea turned to go.

And nearly fell back against Lucian's desk. Mattias's grandmother, Dexna, stood behind her with a large book tightly clutched in her hands. She was staring into Thea's face with a strange intensity.

"Oh!" Thea said. "Good afternoon. How are you?" She remembered too late that it wasn't polite to ask a question of someone who couldn't answer.

Dexna smiled briefly and nodded. She wore no fur, so she couldn't have just arrived. How had Thea missed her? She was dressed in a light green tunic and leggings, with her hair tied in its usual silver knot.

Dexna just held her book and continued to bore into Thea with her eyes.

"Well," Thea said, "I was just leaving. Good-bye, then."

Outside, Thea flipped down the blades of her skates and tried to remember everything Lucian had said about the tree-sign and the settlement map. Her head was swimming with questions when she turned off the pass onto the Mainway, and it took her several minutes to recognize that she was skating away from home. She laughed at herself; she was already halfway to Mattias.

NINE

PETER

Peter had only the vaguest idea what he was trying to do. He wanted the fluttering to come back, and then whatever came after it. He had spent the morning looking at things. First, he looked out his round window at the snow piled everywhere, then he looked up at the geebee geebee's bright blue ceiling, then at a spoon he had placed in the middle of his bed. A comic book. A compass. A can of Jonas's Danish tea from the kitchen.

He kept his eyes open until they watered. He blinked until he was dizzy. But for the first time in weeks there was no fluttering at all, not even for a moment. What was this thing that crept up on him when he wasn't thinking about it, and then disappeared the minute he went looking for it?

He stood up from his bed and jerked back his curtain to see his mother writing at the table with a distant look on her face. She had her hair in its bun, and her hand moved steadily across the open page of the thick red notebook in front of her. She didn't look up.

Peter had been awakened that morning by the sound of Jonas trying to make coffee in the kitchen—something his mother usually did.

This was how her sadness, her "headaches," always started: She stopped doing the things she had always done, shed her habits like clothes that were suddenly too warm. She should be pestering him about staying in the tent all morning, telling him that the sun was shining, he might at least take Sasha for a walk. But she just sat at the table, writing.

Abruptly, she stopped and stood up. She disappeared into the bunk area she shared with Peter's father, and emerged a minute later with a square box wrapped in pale green paper. She held it out to him. "I nearly forgot. Your Friday present."

That green paper could only have come from one place. But still he couldn't quite believe it. "From Fonel's?"

She smiled. "Open it."

He unwrapped the box and opened it, revealing many,

many chocolate eggs, wrapped in foil of every color. They were Ruby Fonel's spring eggs, his favorite. She made them day and night for a week in March, and then she didn't make any more, even if people came in and begged.

They each took one from the box—Peter a blue egg, his mother dark pink—and then she returned to her red notebook. She wrote intently for some minutes before breaking off and staring into space.

Peter had a few more eggs. It was weird how just seeing the familiar colors could make him feel so homesick for New York. He wondered what Miles was doing. Sasha raised her snout from the floor and sniffed. He kept her mostly inside with him now.

"They look pretty darn good, don't they, Sasha?" Peter said. He was testing: The mother in his mind called out from the table, "Chocolate is poison to dogs, Peter. Don't even let her lick your fingers!" But the one at the table was silent.

He sat up and stuffed his feet into the boots that sat on the floor next to his bed. Sasha looked up at him hopefully. "No chocolate for you, girl. Wanna take a walk?"

Outside, the sky was nearly cloudless and the glare hurt his eyes, but he decided not to go back for his goggles. He stopped at the research tent, where his father and Jonas sat in their coats at a small folding table, typing on two laptop computers.

"Hey, Pete." But his father had hardly looked up before he was typing again.

"Shouldn't you guys be out looking at some ice somewhere?" Peter asked. "I'm pretty sure you could be doing this in New York."

Jonas smiled and waved his fingers at Peter. "But in New York we wouldn't be wearing gloves."

"Right," Peter said. "Well, Sasha's waiting for me outside."

"Looking for the Second Volkswagen Road again?" Jonas asked.

"No, just a walk."

"Don't give up," Jonas said, squinting at a sheet of numbers. "It's out there."

"Okay." Peter unzipped the tent flap to go out.

He walked west, toward the ice wall. Sasha trotted along beside him, her tail waving happily. Then she stopped, tensed for a moment, and tore ahead. Peter saw her freeze again, then turn around and streak back to him. She galloped around him, tearing off into the distance and then circling back before running hard again. She ran, circled back to him, ran, circled back.

At first he thought she was running for the joy of it. But then he saw that each time she took off, she ran in the same direction, covering her own tracks in the snow with new prints: She was trying to lead him to something.

"Sasha?"

She ran ahead again, then circled back to him.

"What is it, girl?" Peter shaded his eyes with one gloved hand and looked in the direction of the not-yet-visible wall. There was nothing to see but blue sky meeting shining white snow. He squinted.

It started in just a few seconds: a shimmering that could have been sunlight playing tricks, but wasn't. Peter's heart gave a quiet leap. He stayed as still as he could, and Sasha held still next to him. He kept his eyes on the horizon, drew it toward him.

A moment later the ice wall was in front of him, gleaming in the sunlight. His eyes found the red ring, no bigger than a quarter, and focused on it. The ring came closer until he could see it clearly, twisting strands of color suspended in the ice. He stared at it, careful not to bring it too close this time.

And then, just to the side of the wall, he saw something else: movement. At first it was difficult to see exactly what it was that was moving; Peter figured later that it was because he was seeing white against white— white ground, white ice, big white bear. Peter's blood went hot at the sight of it. There was a polar bear lumbering around out there, and Sasha had been trying to lead him straight to it.

The bear's body was huge and rounded, cartoonish even. The bear walked a bit, then stopped, walked a bit, then stopped. It took Peter another minute to see the cub

115

walking behind it—a smaller white form, with the same black stuffed-animal eyes as its mother. He watched them until he felt something behind his eyes begin to throb. Then he closed his eyes, reached for whatever muscle he was using, and tried to release it.

When he opened his eyes, he saw nothing: blackness. Don't panic, he told himself. There had been moments like this before. He squatted and touched the cold ground. He felt Sasha rub up against him. And then he could see—light was everywhere; it surrounded him in daggers. He raised his head: The horizon was empty again. He put his face into Sasha's neck fur and inhaled. His head pounded.

"You're a good hunter. But no more bears, okay, girl?" He stood slowly and held her collar. With only a few backward glances, Sasha let him lead her back to camp.

He was reluctant to walk past the silent research tent to the geebee geebee, where he was sure he would find his mother just as he had left her. Maybe Jonas would have time for another dogsledding lesson. He was getting better.

But when he had grunted his way up the short slope, he found Jonas knee-deep in the snow between the geebee geebee and the dogs' house. Building an igloo.

"My grandfather and I built one every summer when I came to visit," Jonas called as he used his knife to pry a rectangular block from the snow, "even if we had to hike awhile to find the right kind of snow." He had finished one circle of blocks, and was working on a second level.

"You're leaving a lot of spaces in between," Peter said. "Kind of drafty."

Jonas laughed, slicing into the snowbank with his knife again.

"It's supposed to look like that. I'll pack the holes in with loose snow later."

"Oh. So, are you moving in here or something?"

Jonas looked up. "Not at all. This is just for fun. Temporary housing. Most Inuit use them on hunting trips. They build a new igloo every night—kind of like putting up a tent. I might spend a night in it, though. Want to help me build?"

They finished the igloo together. Jonas stacked the blocks in ever-smaller circles while Peter scooped up armfuls of snow and patched up the spaces between them. When they had a nice tight dome about four feet high, they stood back and admired it. Peter was a little disappointed to finish so quickly.

Then he burst out laughing. "Um, Jonas? I think we forgot something. How are we going to get in?"

Jonas scratched his head and walked around the igloo a few times pretending to look for a door, then admitted that it was supposed to be left for last. He let Peter cut the archway, which turned out lopsided but usable, and together they cleared the snow from the new entrance. Then Jonas got down on all fours to go inside, and Peter crawled in after him.

"Cozy," he said, although it occurred to him that it might get chilly sitting around on the snow.

Jonas straightened up halfway and began boring a little hole through the roof. "For light, and to let the warm air out," he explained. "And if we're really going to do this right, we should build a tunnel in front of the entrance to protect us from the wind."

Peter grinned. "Let's do it."

Using smaller blocks this time, they made an arched tunnel about as long as Peter's body, just high enough to crawl through.

"This is where the orphans used to sleep," Jonas said, as they were wiggling through it. "Their bodies blocked the wind for the others."

"The orphans? You mean kids?"

"Yes, kids. Life was tough for them. They usually had to fight with the dogs for scraps after everyone had shared out the meat."

"God, that's awful," Peter said, now sitting cross-legged inside the dome, where the bright point of light over his head was the only sign of the sunny day outside.

"Yes and no," Jonas said. "Those children got strong, and they often became the most respected elders of the community. They made very good hunters, because they had learned to withstand cold and starvation."

Peter thought about that. "It still stinks," he said.

"To tell you the truth," Jonas said, "I agree with you. But my grandparents probably wouldn't."

They were quiet until Peter said, "Jonas?"

"Yeah?"

"Do you ever have the feeling that my dad is looking for something? Besides the glacier-type stuff?"

Jonas gave Peter an amused look. "Occasionally, yes."

"I thought so. Any idea what it is?"

"Not yet."

"Want to ask him?"

Jonas smiled. "Not yet."

Peter nodded. "Okay."

"Why don't you ask him?"

Peter thought. "If he were willing to tell me, I think he already would have."

After a few seconds, Jonas said, "Whatever it is, I think your mom is looking for it, too."

TEN

Thea

Thea was on the pass to the waterwheel when she saw Mattias skating in the other direction.

"Mattias!"

He waved and slowed down.

She glanced over her shoulder, saw no one behind her, and made a neat arc to join him. They picked up speed, skating toward the Mainway together.

"Are you through for the day?" Thea asked.

"Just out. But I have to go to my grandmother's for supper."

"Do you have time for a stop? I have something to show you."

Mattias smiled. "Yes." Mattias never looked forward to supper with Dexna.

Thea eyed the blue apprentice's sash Mattias wore. "Can't you stuff that in your bag? It practically glows."

Mattias looked down with a frown.

"Unless you had planned on wearing it to bed." Thea loved to tease him about his fancy engineering apprenticeship.

"You're very funny." Mattias lifted the sash over his head, folded it, and tucked in into his shoulder sack as he skated.

"Are you going to tell me what this is about?" he asked.

"Someone left something in my sleeping chamber during the first-line supper. A map."

Mattias's surprise told Thea that he had known nothing about it.

"What sort of map?"

"It's a copy—a very good copy—of the first settlement map."

"Grace's Hope, you mean?"

"Yes."

"Very strange. Do you have any idea why?"

"None at all."

"I wonder if it has to do with your council address."

"I hadn't thought of that. But what does an old map have to do with it?"

Mattias shook his head. "Dunno."

"I went to the archive today and asked Lucian some questions."

"And?"

"He said that the . . . that the 'traditional interpretation' of the map is wrong. 'Flawed,' he said."

"How can that be? It's a map of Gracehope. How else should we interpret it?"

They came to the Mainway, crowded with skaters.

"We'll talk more when we get there," Thea said quietly.

"Get where?"

"Main Hall. I want to look at the original."

They entered the hall by the side gate, hoping to avoid anyone who might be shopping at the market stalls, and slipped into the exhibition chamber. There was rarely anyone here when classes were out of session, and they were happy to find themselves alone.

"It's over here." The far wall was lined with framed maps. Thea's map was part of a set of four drawn at the same time. The cousins studied them for a while without speaking. Thea saw that the map with the tree-sign was more of a sketch than the other three, which were drawn with great precision. She hadn't remembered that.

"Meriwether always said that this one was intended as an overview," Mattias said, gesturing to Thea's map, "and that these"—he gestured to the others—"were detail studies." Thea never understood how Mattias could miss so many lectures and still seem to know almost everything.

It was true that the other maps in the set were much more detailed: the largest, a map of the original settlement homes, showed each set of chambers distinctly drawn and labeled. Thea could find her own sleeping chamber on it if she took the time.

A second map showed the waterwheel and the enormous council chamber. The third was a careful treatment of the lake, showing every curve and dip of the shoreline.

Only Thea's map showed everything together. Next to the others, it seemed almost freely drawn, things sketched in without a care for scale or exact position.

Mattias squinted at the wall. "Let's start with fundamentals. Why is this map so roughly drawn while the others are so detailed?"

"Because it shows an overview?"

Mattias nodded. "According to Meriwether, yes. But maybe Meriwether is wrong. Isn't that what Lucian said?"

Thea wished she could remember exactly what Lucian had said. "I think so." She looked and looked at the map, waiting for something to happen. "Mattias," she said after a minute. "There is one detail. Look at the lake."

She pointed. Gracehope's lake had a deep crack running along one icy shore and into the water. It was through this fissure that gases escaped from the earth into the depths of the water, warming it.

"The fissure is drawn very carefully," Thea said. "See how it bends just a little there? That's just exactly how it goes. Why bother to get it so exactly right, if this map is no more than a sketch?"

Mattias nodded. "Good. And why include the migration tunnel? These maps weren't supposed to be historical documents—they're practically blueprints of the original settlement. They were meant to be used. And the tunnel was long reclaimed by the time they were drawn."

"And why does this map alone show the sun-sign and the tree-sign?" Thea asked.

Mattias narrowed his eyes. "The sun-sign is a symbol of the wider world. Tell me again what Lucian said about the tree-sign."

"It means something like 'survival.' "

Mattias had been looking intently at the map while they spoke. Now he turned to her, his green eyes wide. "What if this isn't a map of the settlement at all? What if it's a map of the tunnel?"

Thea's heart began to pound. "How do you mean?"

Mattias pointed. "Look here. Anybody knows that the migration tunnel led from the surface to the lakeshore. But this shows exactly *where* it ended—it's drawn to just where the lake fissure bends near the shore. I know exactly the place it means."

Thea nodded. "So do I." After a minute, she pointed at the map's faded tree-sign. "Lucian said that in the old world, the tree symbol had a literal translation—'one survives.' "

"One survives," Mattias repeated numbly.

"Mattias." Thea grasped his wrist. "The tunnel is still there."

"We're just making guesses," Mattias said quickly. "We don't know we're right."

"Someone is showing us the way. But who?"

"You're rushing to conclusions, Thea."

"Am I? Why was the map left for me, then?"

"How do I know? Maybe it's someone's idea of a joke."

"There's too much effort in it—the paper, the ink. And anyway, it isn't remotely funny. Mattias, we have to find out if it's true."

"How are we supposed to do that?"

"You have some handblowers at the waterwheel, don't you?"

"I hope you're joking. If Berling ever found out I took a blower . . ."

"We'll borrow it late at night and have it back before first light."

"No. And I should go now—I have to get to my grand-mother's."

"Mattias!"

"What?"

Thea stared at him.

Mattias sighed. "Let me think about it," he said as he started for the door.

"All right, just think about it," Thea said, catching up.

The long spiral of the Mainway was almost empty by the time they neared the old quarter. They were alone as they started around the final arc of the passage.

"Do you think tomorrow night is a possibility?" Thea kept her voice low.

"Tomorrow!" Mattias's eyes stayed on the ground in front of him.

"Why wait? Aren't you excited, Mattias? If we're right about this, it . . . it changes everything."

"I suppose."

"You *suppose*?"

"What you're suggesting . . . it might be dangerous, Thea, and not just for us. Have you even thought of that?"

"But what about the expansion? We've talked about it a hundred times."

"That was talking. Because *you* wanted to talk about it. This is different. What if we're right? We should tell someone. Maybe I should talk to Chief Berling."

"No. The map was left in secret for a reason. First let's see if the passage is there."

Mattias didn't answer, and for the first time Thea wondered: *Was* she being thoughtless? She only wanted what

Mai had wanted. Hadn't her mother risked everything? Hadn't Grace?

The light was dimmed now; soft green and orange lights burned in globes outside the doors they passed. As they drew closer to the chambers Dexna shared with Rowen, Thea saw that the wooden door was slightly ajar. Orange light spilled onto the pass from inside.

She heard Rowen's voice, and put a warning arm in front of Mattias.

Rowen's words became clear as they glided to the open door, their skates nearly silent on the ice.

". . . purpose does it serve?" Rowen asked angrily. "You never have an answer to that, do you? And you fail to accept that it is not your place . . ."

Rowen stood just inside the door in her skates and outerwrap. Seeing Mattias and Thea, she stepped onto the pass and pushed away without another word. She even skated angrily, Thea thought as she watched Rowen disappear around the bend.

When Thea peeked inside the door, Dexna was standing in the middle of the greatroom, her face flushed. How could anyone argue with her?

Dexna beckoned them both inside.

"Thank you," Thea said quickly, "but I must get home. Lana will worry." She leaned toward Mattias. "Meet me in the dogs' shelter after supper. Please."

ELEVEN

PETER

Peter's feet were cold, and the glare of sun on snow made his eyes burn. He watched his father fiddle with some dials on an Automatic Weather Station, which turned out to be a fancy name for a pole stuck in the snow with a bunch of equipment hanging off it— there were two solar panels, a battery, and a bunch of little black boxes that recorded temperature and snowfall and about nine other things.

The station was put up by someone else years before, and Peter's dad and Jonas had come to make sure it hadn't blown over or been buried by snow. Peter had driven the sled most of the way. Rocketing along with the dogs fanned out in front of him, he was happy. He didn't think about his mother looking sad or his father being distracted all the time. His mind felt empty. He just flew.

Stopping had been a problem—they overshot the weather station and had to circle back—but his father thumped him on the back and Jonas said he was making real progress.

Jonas checked the last little black box, wrote some things down in his notebook, and then sighed and grabbed a shovel from the sled.

"Time to start digging the snow pit. I thought the wind might die down," he muttered.

"Want some help?" Peter asked.

"Nah, we'd only whack each other with the shovels. It's a one-man job."

So Peter sat on the sled, rubbed Sasha's belly, and watched Jonas dig a neat square in the snow. With almost every shovelful, the wind blew loose snow back into his face. Jonas grimaced but kept going.

Peter's mother was off on her own somewhere today—she had already left the geebee geebee when Peter woke up that morning. His dad said she had gone for a walk to think about her book.

Jonas dug and dug. The pit took shape: It was about a four-foot square, and Jonas was up to his neck in it. Finally, he called Peter's father over to look.

"Great," Dr. Solemn said. "Chart it."

After all of that work, Peter thought his dad could have come up with something more enthusiastic, but Jonas didn't seem to mind. He smiled at Peter and pulled two Hershey bars out of a coat pocket.

"All done. Care to celebrate with me?"

When they had eaten the candy, Jonas went to his pack, pulled out a notebook and a pen, and hopped into the hole. Peter helped by borrowing the measuring tape from his father and holding it at the top edge of the pit. Jonas pulled the tape down to the floor. He pushed his goggles onto his forehead and squinted at the wall of the pit.

"What are you looking for?" Peter asked.

"Lots of things," Jonas said. "I've dug through about a year of snowfall, and first I'm looking for blue streaks of ice—they might show when there was a big storm, compacting the snow into ice, or they might indicate where snow melted and then froze into ice."

He began to sketch the wall in his notebook. "I'm also looking at the size of the snow grains, and I'm noting how densely the snow is packed. See, this snow up top is pretty loosely packed—we call that 'fist' because I can shove my fist right into it. Then there's 'four fingers,' 'two fingers,' 'one finger,' 'pencil,' and 'knife.' Not so technical, right? But it works. Jump down here and I'll show you."

Peter slid into the hole.

"Give it a try." Jonas pointed to a spot near the bottom. "Just push your fist in."

Peter tried. It was like trying to push his fist into a brick wall. He leaned hard, but nothing happened.

"Try a finger."

Nope.

Jonas laughed. "Hard, right? But try this." He pulled a regular yellow pencil from his pocket. Peter pushed it against the wall—it went in.

"Pencil," Jonas wrote.

They finished the job together, measuring and pushing and finding streaks of ice that Jonas copied into his book.

"That was great," Peter said when they had climbed out.

"I'm glad you thought so," Jonas said. "Next time you can dig!"

"So do those notes tell you anything you didn't already know?"

"Only when we look at everything together," Jonas said. "Then we can see patterns: when it snowed, when the temperature rose or dropped, stuff like that."

"But why do you care?"

"You mean, who cares when it snows on a deserted ice cap?" Jonas smiled. "It matters. This ice sheet is about two miles deep, and it's moving."

"I don't really get how it moves."

"When there's icemelt, water slips down into cracks in the ice. Then whole big chunks slip on the water toward the ocean. Some falls in and melts, and the ocean rises."

"That's what Dad is always talking about."

Jonas nodded. "It's a pretty big deal. If the whole Greenland ice cap melted, the ocean would be about twenty feet higher, everywhere, even in New York City."

"I know," Peter said. "Dad says that's why we live on the top floor."

Jonas laughed. "He's a savvy guy, your dad."

Peter drove the sled home, and the dogs stopped on a dime. His mother came in while they were making lunch. She gave Peter a hug, and he felt her shake her head over his shoulder at his dad.

After lunch, Jonas and Dr. Solemn disappeared into the research tent. Peter's mother sat at the table with her red notebook, and Peter settled into bed with a stack of comic books. After about an hour there was a long sigh from the table.

He watched his mother stretch and gather herself, as if she were remembering where all of her body parts were located. She put her elbows on the table and looked at

Peter on his bed. "Do you have homework to do? I could help you."

"Homework?" Peter said. "I'm way ahead already."

"Oh." She considered him. "We should have brought you some radio kits," she said slowly. "I don't know why we didn't think of that." He hated the way she was talking, as if she were pushing her words through layers and layers of something—cloth, or fog, or mud.

"Me neither," he said.

They were quiet for a minute.

"Well," his mother said, as if that one word cost her untold amounts of energy, "do you feel like learning something about science?"

"Right now, you mean?"

"If you want to."

"Why not." Anything to separate her from that red notebook for a while. Anything to wake her up.

He took a few chocolate eggs from the box next to his bed and joined her at the table, where she closed the notebook and pushed it to one side. Sasha hopped up to follow him and then settled herself again at their feet.

His mother said, "Do you remember what mitochondria are?"

"The cell's engines," Peter droned. He'd been hearing the same definition from her since he was five.

"Yes," she said with a half-smile. "I guess it's time we got past that."

133

She seemed to be reviving. Something inside him lifted a little.

"Mitochondria *are* like engines," his mother said, "because they burn energy. But they're engines that build themselves. They come with their own set of instructions—DNA."

"I know what DNA is, Mom."

"You've learned about *nuclear* DNA. Nuclear DNA is like instructions to the cells, or a blueprint, explaining how to build the human body. I'm talking about mitochondrial DNA, which tells each cell's *engine* how to build itself so that the cell can do the work it's supposed to do. Different cells do different work—brain cells do brain work, muscle cells do muscle work. Am I going too fast?"

She sounded more and more like herself. "No, I'm getting it," Peter said. "The engines build themselves, and the cells use the engines to burn energy and do their work. Hearing, thinking, moving a muscle, whatever."

His mother nodded. "Good. When cells divide to make new cells—it's happening all the time—the mitochondrial DNA, or mtDNA for short, is copied, over and over. Every new cell needs its own mtDNA, so that it can build itself an engine. Still with me? Okay then, here's the tricky part.

"As the mtDNA—the engine-building instructions—is being copied, changes can occur. Unintended changes, called mutations. And these mutations will change the kind of engine that will be built, just as different sets of instructions will build different radios. Most of the changes are very small, something like coiling the radio wire clockwise instead of counterclockwise around the spool. It shouldn't make a big difference, but sometimes it does."

Peter nodded. He'd built enough radios to know.

"Well, I study those mutations in mtDNA, and how they affect the way people develop. Have you ever heard of Leber's disease?"

Peter shook his head.

"Leber's disease impairs vision, and causes blindness in some people. And the disease is caused by one base change to the mtDNA."

"Base change?"

"Think of it as a one-word change in a set of radio-kit instructions. 'Twist' instead of 'rotate,' something like that. With mtDNA, this one base change makes the cell's engine a little less efficient, a little less powerful. That's fine for some sorts of cells, because some cells don't need a strong engine—skin cells, for example."

Peter considered his skin. It didn't seem to be doing much.

"But other sorts of cells have harder jobs to do. The cells of the optic nerve, for example, need a great deal of energy. So a less powerful engine makes it hard for them to function properly. And that's what Leber's disease is: A mutation in the mtDNA makes the engine a little less efficient, and vision problems occur because the cells of the optic nerve aren't making enough power."

Vision problems, Peter thought. Was she trying to tell him something?

"So," he said slowly, "if the cell's engine is less efficient, some things won't work as well as they should."

"Right. High-energy cells need strong engines—cells of the auditory pathway for hearing, and brain cells, and cells of certain internal organs. And these are all the things we see affected by mtDNA mutations. Muscle tissue also needs a lot of energy. There's something called ragged red disease that results in muscle weakness instead of vision problems."

Peter nodded, his toes buried in Sasha's fur under the table. He was flooded for a moment by happiness—his mother was back. She was right there with him. "That's cool, Mom. So you're writing about all of those diseases?"

She shook her head. "No, those have been written about already. I'm studying other kinds of mutations. I'm looking at what might happen if the mtDNA accidentally *improved* through mutation, and the cell engines became more efficient, instead of less."

"Like extra-powerful engines?"

"Yes."

"Does that ever happen?"

Mrs. Solemn smiled another real smile. "No one knows for sure. But I think it's possible."

Peter glanced at the pad on which his mother had been doodling while she spoke.

He caught his breath, then jabbed the middle of the page with two fingers. "What's that supposed to be?"

She looked down at the paper as if she were seeing it for the first time.

"That's mitochondrial DNA. It's twisted, in a ring."

TWELVE

THEA

After supper, Thea stroked Peg's ears and waited for Mattias. Before long, he ducked inside the dogs' shelter. "All right," he said. "Tonight, then."

She sat up. "Really?"

"Chief Berling has a late meeting with Rowen. I was with him when the messenger came. I'll meet you at the waterwheel. We'll borrow a blower and go to the lake. The lake path is dark after last light; with hope, no one will be anywhere near it."

Tonight. She stared at him.

"Do you want to do this or not?"

"Yes!"

"If I don't have the blower back by first light, Berling will never want to see me again."

"I know."

"Eleven o'clock. Bring a sleigh, and Peg and Gru. The blower is heavy." He started to leave.

"Mattias . . . Thank you," Thea said. But Mattias said nothing.

Lana was long asleep when Thea called Peg and Gru, keeping her voice low so she wouldn't wake Lynx, Rowen's companion, or any of the other older Chikchu. Thea crouched next to the dock and harnessed the dogs to her sleigh. She had piled every fur she had onto it, along with a lightglobe and a water sack. They sped along the deserted backways to the waterwheel. She loved being out late, when it was almost dark. The dogs knew the pathways well enough to run with their eyes closed. The thrumming of the waterwheel grew louder as they drew close.

Mattias was already there, looking grim. He and Ham stood at the edge of the waterwheel's courtyard with a water blower on the ground between them. It was heavy. Together, they loaded it onto the sleigh and covered it with Thea's furs. Neither of them spoke. Mattias harnessed Ham to Thea's sleigh, and they set off for the lake.

Thea drove the sleigh along the lake path until they saw the deep crack in the shoreline. "Here," Mattias said.

He stepped off the sleigh and examined the wall beside them. It looked perfectly smooth. Then he took a special marker from his coat and began to draw.

"Mattias! Do you think you should?"

He laughed quietly. "Didn't you ask me to help you blow a *hole* in this wall?"

Thea felt silly.

"Don't worry," Mattias said. "We use these at the waterwheel. It rubs off."

When he was finished, they struggled with the water blower, supporting it together. Thea fought to keep the powerful stream of water within the crude circle Mattias had drawn on the ice wall in front of them. The water ran down the wall and into the lake. A messy hole grew in the wall.

When the hole was so deep that they could no longer see the back of it, they stopped. Mattias reached his arm in nearly up to the shoulder, then shook his head. "I can still feel ice back there," he said. Thea thought she saw relief flash across his face.

She took off her gloves and stroked Peg. It felt good to flex her cramped hands. Ham and Gru were a few feet away, next to the sleigh piled high with furs.

"Maybe we're looking in the wrong place," Thea ventured.

But they both knew that if the map was telling them what they thought it was telling them, the tunnel should be here. The bend in the lakeside fissure was just yards from where they stood, and it pointed to this spot on the wall.

"We'll keep going," Mattias said, hoisting the blower again.

Thea hoped that their dimmed lightglobe couldn't be seen through the trees from the Mainway. Someone was sure to pass eventually, despite the hour.

Peg signaled: *Four blades.*

Thea had just enough time to black the lightglobe before two skaters fairly flew past the lake on the Mainway. Mattias sighed loudly in the dark as Thea rekindled the lantern—even dimmer now.

"Stop worrying," she said, taking up the blower again. "You'll probably be in bed within the hour. Now aim."

Something gave way almost as soon as they began. They heard chunks of ice fall into an opening behind the wall. Thea's stomach turned over.

Mattias stopped the blower and put it down carefully. "Could be an air pocket."

"It isn't, and you know it." Thea was surprised to hear her voice shaking.

"I'll take a look." Mattias picked up the lantern and, bracing himself with one knee, swung it gently into the hole by its woven strap. He leaned in after it, wiggling through the hole until Thea could see nothing but his knees and feet. Then he was still.

"Mattias?" Thea whispered. "What do you see?"

He struggled out again. Without a word, he waved Thea up toward the opening. His expression was hard to read.

Thea put her arms through the hole and inched herself through the tight space toward the lantern's glow on the other side.

It was there: smooth walls leading straight away from her. A passage, wide enough to fit a sleigh and a team. A door to the wider world, and she'd been walking past it her whole life.

They hadn't talked about what they'd do if they found it. But Thea knew as soon as she saw the pathway disappearing into darkness in front of her. Her heart banging, she squirmed her way out and faced Mattias. "I'm going in."

"Take the lantern and stand back," he said, raising the blower again. "I'll try to make the hole big enough to fit the sleigh through, but I warn you I won't run the blower dry. We may need it again."

We. Thea smiled. He was coming with her.

In a few moments, the hole was big enough to step through easily. Mattias went first, with the lantern, then Peg, Gru, and Ham, boosted up by Thea, followed by the sleigh, the blower, and finally Thea, with her water sack slung over one shoulder. They had to be back well before first light; there was not much time.

With the dogs harnessed and everything tied down on the sleigh, Thea signaled Peg to lead them. But they had taken no more than two steps when Gru gave a sharp bark and stalked to the lead position. Peg fell back next to Ham.

"Strange," said Thea. "Gru always lets Peg lead." There was no question of Ham's leading. Though he was the largest of the three animals, he had no interest in telling others what to do.

Mattias had fastened the dimmed lantern to the front of the sleigh. Something stopped Thea from telling him to brighten it. It may have been the look on his face. Mattias was scared.

Thea had imagined that the tunnel would climb sharply, like the steep steps to the balcony in the council chamber, but for some time they walked on level ground. Then, hardly realizing it at first, they began to ascend.

Although she had traveled in the dark many times on the backways, the closeness of the space and the flickering of the lightglobe made Thea uneasy. She kept one hand on Mattias and trailed the other along the smooth tunnel wall. The slope became gradually steeper until they walked with effort.

Then Thea gave a yell, gripping Mattias's arm tighter and pulling him close. There were drawings on the walls. Detailed figures walked alongside dogs and sleighs heaped with bundles. The images were shockingly familiar: The faces from the walls of the council chamber. These were the Settlers, walking down into their new land. But they weren't the icy figures she had grown accustomed to—here there was color.

"This one's Sarah!" she said. Her foremother wore fur pants and a green tunic that showed under her fur jacket. Sarah looked much happier here than she did on the council chamber wall, her cheeks bright as she smiled down at the Chikchu next to her. "Look, Mattias! Here's Sarah's companion—four white feet!"

"Thea!" Mattias shouted. He pulled her to the other side of the tunnel, where more figures were visible in the dim glow.

Thea looked closely at the painted figures, but she didn't recognize any of these faces. Mattias loosened the sleigh's straps and removed the lightglobe from its tight nest of furs. He held it up to the wall.

There were so many of them, every face a fresh one—there were babies wrapped in colored cloth and held by their mothers, children carrying Chikchu pups, older men and women riding on sleighs, their backs straight and long. Lots of people.

"It doesn't make sense," Mattias said after a while.

"What doesn't?"

"Who are the babies?"

Mattias was right. There were no babies among the Settlers. Nor were there many old people. These people couldn't be Settlers. She glanced behind her, to Sarah and the others, and realized what they had missed.

"Mattias."

"What?"

"The Settlers are walking down."

"And?"

"The Settlers are walking to Gracehope."

Mattias followed her gaze to the Settlers on the other side of the tunnel, then back to the wall in front of them, where children held hands and mothers held babies and clusters of young men walked together. There were so many of them, and every one of them was headed in the same direction.

Up.

To the wider world.

This was how the Settlers saw the future. It was how Sarah had imagined . . . imagined *her,* Thea realized.

Mattias was silent. He walked a few steps away from her and then came back, the lantern raised in one hand. "Do you know what this means?" he said quietly.

"The Settlers meant for us to leave."

"Grace's hope." Mattias said. Thea's mind conjured an image of the map that lay safely in her trunk at home, the two words written in flowery letters across the top: Grace's Hope. Gracehope. We have it all wrong, she thought.

Water. Peg's signal came out of the darkness just in

front of them. It took Thea a few extra moments to absorb her meaning.

Water, Peg signaled again.

"The dogs are thirsty," Thea murmured absently to Mattias. He was at the wall again, moving the lantern from figure to figure as he examined them.

A moment later, water was rushing over their booted feet, flowing down the tunnel from somewhere above them. Cold water. In a few moments it was ankle-deep.

THIRTEEN

PETER

Peter woke to the sound of his mother calling out in her sleep.

"No!" she said loudly. And then, "Because it's *gone*."

His father was whispering. "Rory, you're dreaming. Wake up, Rory."

The night was overcast—Peter could barely see his hand in front of his face. He flipped onto his side with a jerk, pulling his blanket tightly around him.

"I'm trying to make sense of it." His mother's voice, awake now. Agitated.

"I know you are, my love."

"It's disappeared, hasn't it?"

There was a pause, and then Peter heard his father's voice again, very low now. "Perhaps. Though I don't see how."

"Are we too late?"

"No, not too late."

Peter wondered what Jonas was making of this, and then remembered he was sleeping in the igloo tonight.

"Find it for me, Gregory."

"Shhh." Peter could imagine his father smoothing his mother's hair.

"Don't shush me," she said, and then there were no more words.

Peter reached out into the darkness with one arm. His hand found the knob of the drawer where he had hidden his mother's drawing. He gripped it tightly, trying to decide whether to pull. He didn't want his parents to know he was awake. His father would feel compelled to come and tell him everything was fine.

He heard the clicking of Sasha's nails on the floor, coming toward him. She walked around at night sometimes, moving from post to post according to her own agenda. Now she lay down next to Peter's bed and began licking his hand. His fingers were covered in wet warmth. He released the knob and pushed his hand into her fur.

A bit of starlight shone faintly through his window, and he could see Sasha's face resting on her paws below him. The clouds were clearing off.

Tomorrow, he told himself.

FOURTEEN

THEA

"What's happening? Where's the water coming from?" Thea slipped, jostling the sleigh. Still harnessed to the three Chikchu, it hardly moved. But the heavy blower, freed from the straps that Mattias had loosened to retrieve the lantern, toppled from its perch, slid down the steep slope of wet ice, and disappeared from view.

Mattias let out a long, low noise, echoed by a cry of concern from Ham so sharp that Thea covered her ears.

"It isn't safe to be here without a blower, Thea. We have to go down after it. Now."

150

Thea shook her head. "There isn't time. The blower has to be back at the waterwheel before first light. It will be waiting for us at the bottom. I'm going up."

"Thea," Mattias said in a grave voice. "No one knows where we are. This water will turn to ice down below. We could be shut out within hours, with no way back in."

"The water might stop at any time. I'm going up while I can."

Mattias grasped one of her wrists. "It's not going to stop. Our hole must have created an air current that diverted this icemelt from another path. We have to go back down before it seals us out. Now."

"Mattias, think. Think of what is up there: the sun, the sky, the 'horizon' that you've tried to explain to me so many times. I need to see it. Don't you?"

"Maybe I don't need to see it. Maybe I'm not like you, Thea!"

"Go back if you want to, then. I'm going to the surface. I think we're close."

Peg seemed to agree. *Air,* she observed.

"We have to stay together," Mattias said. He drew a long breath and let it out. "If I go to the top with you, will you come straight back down? Right away?"

Thea grinned with relief and excitement and held up one hand. "On my line, Mattias."

They started climbing the path again, as quickly as they could with the water rushing over their feet. The sleigh was much lighter without the blower, and they moved quickly, Mattias holding the lightglobe, its netting wrapped tightly around his wrist.

They didn't speak, concentrating on their steps, Thea anticipating the wider world while she knew that Mattias fretted over the one that awaited their return. The path was steep, and she could hear herself breathing hard. She slipped once or twice, but caught herself before she fell. Finally, she felt the quality of the air changing, ever so slightly.

Air, Peg offered again.

Mattias appeared to notice the change as well. He held the lightglobe up a little higher. He was breathless and looked scared again; she slipped her hand into his.

Three minutes later, they stood gasping in front of an archway. And on the other side of it was the wider world.

It was mostly dark. Thea felt something drop heavily inside her. She had so hoped to see the sun.

The archway stood no higher than the rest of the tunnel, barely three hand-lengths above their heads. It was roughly cut, and when Mattias raised the lamp two words were visible just above their heads.

Hope lives.

Thea realized that Gru was trembling, and bent to

comfort her. Then, no longer feeling the cold water that soaked their boots, she and Mattias stepped together into the darkest hours of an April night.

Thea almost tripped over Gru, who was suddenly between her feet, pulling hard to the right. Thea grabbed the dog's collar.

"Watch out." Mattias's eyes were keener than most. Despite the darkness, he saw that they were at the top of a steep slope, on a lip of frozen earth not much wider than their sleigh. Stretching one arm around Thea's shoulders, he peered into the night. "Right or left?"

Thea looked down at Gru. "I don't think she'll *go* left," she said.

"Then we'll go right."

There was a cluster of high ridges in the ice, each about the height of a man. The cousins wove their way through them carefully until they reached an empty space where the flat edge of the slope broadened a little. Mattias relaxed his grip on Thea.

The vastness made Thea's legs feel weak. She tipped her head back: There was nothing, absolutely nothing, above her. She had a brief sensation of lifting off the ground, as if she might just float up into the sky. She stood on the ice, marveling that it could be both light and dark at the same time, blackest night lit by an infinity of stars.

She heard both nothing and everything—it was as if the very air were crackling around her. She looked at Mattias and smiled. He smiled back.

She freed the dogs from their leads, and Gru immediately began to pace around the small space with her nose to the ground.

Mattias turned his face to the sky. "Look!" he said. "It's Leo."

Thea looked to where he pointed. At first she didn't see how Mattias could distinguish any kind of pattern among the masses of light points above her. Then, as if someone threw a switch in her brain, she began to recognize star patterns.

"Hercules!" she shouted, loving the way her words were absorbed by the air.

The cousins called names back and forth to each other, laughing as each of them recognized another group of stars.

"Ursa Major!"

"Lyra!"

Peg and Ham settled themselves into one furry bundle and fell asleep.

Thea nearly fell over them, and laughed. "Well, they're certainly comfortable. You see, Gru, everything is fine. You can stop your pacing now." But Gru continued to walk the perimeter of the clearing, her ears forward and an occasional whine escaping her throat.

Thea stood still and enjoyed the movement of the air against her face until Mattias said, "It's time, Thea."

She realized with a start that the stars had begun to fade. Yes, it was time to go. She had so much to tell everyone! But she would return, soon enough.

They roused Peg and Ham and attached their sleigh traces. Thea called Gru to her and stroked the Chikchu for a few moments before putting her in the lead position, but Gru wouldn't settle. I shouldn't have brought her, Thea thought. The poor thing has been through enough for one lifetime.

Thea and Mattias picked their way along the narrow edge of the slope, the Chikchu following with the sleigh. They were nearly to the tunnel when Thea heard a short whine behind her and turned to see that Peg had a foot tangled in the sleigh traces. She dropped back, bending to free the dog.

When she stood up, Mattias was gone.

"Mattias!" Thea called. Could he have ducked into the tunnel ahead of her? But she had looked down for only a few seconds. More than that, it was something he would never do.

"Mattias!"

Nothing.

She knew that she should turn her head. She should look to the right, to where the ground fell away from them into darkness. Instead she looked at the dogs. They appeared frozen, as still and lifeless as the Settlers who circled the walls of the council chamber. They were listening.

Then Ham started barking frantically. The sound of it was shocking—the air seemed to soak up the noise and throw it back out again, louder. Thea's ears rang painfully. She squeezed past Peg and released Ham from the sleigh with one hand.

"Find him, Ham. Find Mattias."

FIFTEEN

PETER

It was still a little dark when Peter woke again. The tent was silent. He dressed quietly while Sasha looked on expectantly. He had decided not to bother with a team. The ice wall was not so far.

It took him a minute to find the notepad in the dim kitchen. He wrote "went for an early walk" and left the note on the table. He planned to be back before anyone was up. If not, well, they wouldn't be happy, but they would have to live with it. He filled a canteen and grabbed his knapsack.

Outside, he hitched Sasha to the sled. They walked past Jonas's igloo, where there was no sign of life.

Sasha cantered eagerly toward the ice wall, pulling the sled while Peter ran behind it with his mother's drawing in one coat pocket and a handful of chocolate eggs in the other. He half-doubted his memory of the ring in the ice. Maybe in ordinary weather, he told himself, the thing would look ordinary.

The sky was still half dark but clear, and the cold air stung his nose and his lungs. He felt his body shedding the warmth of bed and sleep, as if he were letting go of something heavy. He ran harder, feeling lighter and happier, flying away from his mother's sadness and his father's worry and the smothering dark of the tent. He didn't want anything holding him down. He resisted the temptation to take off his coat and fling it away from him.

He kept his eyes on Sasha, watching the way her front legs pulled the ground under her and then her back legs pushed it away. He tried in vain to match her stride for stride, his legs moving so quickly it was hard to stay on top of them. He breathed fast and hard; the cold filled him up and burned.

And then they were there, at the ice wall, standing in front of the red ring. He looked.

There was nothing ordinary about it.

SIXTEEN

THEA

Thea watched Ham streak over the side of the slope and down away from her. The white patches of his fur flashed a few times in the semi-dark, and then he was gone.

A few moments later, Ham's barking came again, different now, more deliberate. Two barks, then a beat of silence. Two barks, a beat of silence.

A beacon.

"Mattias!" she called.

Two barks, a beat of silence.

She unharnessed Peg and Gru.

Two barks, a beat of silence.

She turned the sleigh toward the sound and pushed it to the edge of the slope. She lay down on it, waited for Ham's next bark, and aimed the sleigh toward it. One push of her legs brought its nose down hard on the icy slope, and she flew down the hill, Gru and Peg running on either side of her.

Ham came into view abruptly, his tail sticking straight out behind him and his face pointed exactly in her direction. The moment she saw him he stopped barking and turned to nose at something on the ice behind him.

It was Mattias. Or rather it was Mattias's head and shoulders. It took Thea a few moments to work out that the rest of him was rooted in the ice somehow. His eyes were closed, his head resting to one side.

"Mattias!" She touched him. He was warm, alive. Ham walked a slow circle around him, while Gru and Peg sat quietly at a distance, as if they knew Ham was at risk in some way they were not. This, more than anything, scared her.

"Wake up, Mattias!" Thea rubbed his shoulders, his cheeks, the back of his neck. Nothing.

"Mattias, I need to talk to you!" She crouched, grasped him under the arms, and pulled uselessly. "Mattias, Mattias," she chanted. She took off her gloves and felt the ice around him, meeting sharp edges everywhere, nothing like the tame ice she knew. She decided to risk a light.

She groped among the furs heaped on the sleigh, feeling for the lamp. Where was it? She plunged her hands in again and again, desperate. She heard a noise—a sudden heaving sound. Mattias was waking! And then she realized she was hearing her own sobs. The lantern. Where was the lantern?

When she found it, the light didn't show her anything encouraging. There was a long thin crack in the icebed, and Mattias's lower body was jammed into it. She had to wake him. She set the lamp to its brightest and put it down on the ice next to Mattias. Then she slapped his cheeks, pinched his shoulders, and shouted his name into both of his ears until he moved, one jerk of the head, a reflexive action. A few moments later, his eyes opened.

Thea felt her chest expand as if she had just then learned to take in air.

"Mattias. You've fallen. We have to get you out of here. Can you move your legs?"

Mattias shook his head.

"Can you feel your legs, Mattias?" A grim question, but she had to ask.

A moment passed. Mattias nodded.

"Good. That's good."

But she still had no way to get him out.

Mattias was closing his eyes again.

"No, Mattias!" She took his face in her hands. "You have to fight this. Help me get you out of there. I'm going to try to lift you, but I need your help—push away from the ground, Mattias, with your arms. I'll count to three and we'll both—"

"Can't," he said simply. And Thea felt his head go heavy in her hands.

"Mattias!" She tried again to rouse him. She did everything she could short of hurting him, and then she did try to hurt him, pinching him hard, but there was no flicker of consciousness.

She forced her arms under his. She would pull him free. If she could just hold him and stand, he would be free of it. This would be over, Mattias would be himself again, and they would be home. She knew that people could sometimes do extraordinary things at extraordinary moments. Moments like this one. She would stand up with him. This was possible.

Her arms and legs strained against the weight of him, against the ice that fought her for him. She felt the energy flowing out of her—her muscles refusing to yield, giving more than they could really afford to. But she couldn't even begin to stand. Her legs trembled and buckled, and then she was on her knees.

She pounded the ice until her bare hands were

scratched and bleeding. She screamed at it to let Mattias go. Why did it hold him? What use could it have for a boy? "You don't need him!" she cried. She scraped at the icebed around him, hit it with her bloody fists and cried onto it.

She sat beside him for a long time, time she knew she should be using in other ways. The three dogs had silently wrapped themselves around Mattias's shoulders, Ham signaling *home* over and over, looking at her hopefully in the gathering light before he fell asleep with his nose touching Peg's.

She wanted to fall asleep, too. She wanted them all to go away together. But she couldn't sleep. She had to get up and go down the tunnel for help, though she knew Mattias might be dead by the time she got back. There was still a chance, she told herself. There was a chance if she went for help now. But still she didn't move.

The sky lightened slowly until she could see the line of the earth against it.

A horizon. Mattias had tried to explain it to her twenty times, but she had had to see it for herself.

Thea stood, and Gru lifted her head and then got to her feet. Peg and Ham followed her with their eyes but neither made a move to leave Mattias.

"Stay here," Thea told Gru. "Stay with Mattias."

But the Chikchu trotted over to her and cast her eyes up the steep hill that was in front of them. Thea felt

163

herself trembling and realized that she could not drag the sleigh to the top by herself.

"Come on then," she said, hooking Gru's harness to a sleigh trace.

They climbed up the steep slope toward the tunnel entrance, Thea's hands bleeding inside her gloves from the scrapes she'd inflicted while clawing the ice around Mattias. His presence pulled at her from below. She could barely see him now. Ham and Peg had wrapped themselves more tightly around him to cover the ground that Gru had left bare, and his head and shoulders were swaddled in a wealth of black and white fur.

She was nearly to the top of the long slope when Gru began to keen—a piercing, thrumming, vibrating sound, a sound one rarely heard in Gracehope. A sound of alarm. Thea's first thought was that Mattias was dead. But if Mattias had died, it would be Peg and Ham keening. She looked to where the dogs below had raised their heads carefully at Gru's call. Mattias couldn't be dead.

Gru stopped her shrieking for a moment, if only to draw breath, and Thea followed the Chikchu's gaze a little way along the rim of the enormous bowl that held Mattias. A slab of ice jutted out from the crusted earth, still gray-blue in the early morning, but with one edge turning a deep orange. The sun would be rising soon. She tried again to hate everything about this place.

Gru started up again, her gaze never wavering from the

164

ice slab. The sound she made was almost a physical force, pushing Thea away.

"Come on," Thea said to the Chikchu, pulling lightly on her harness strap in the direction of the tunnel. But the dog wouldn't move. Gru's body was rigid.

Thea was afraid. One hand on Gru's neck, she looked toward the ice slab again. Something was moving next to it.

SEVENTEEN

PETER

There it was: a circle of twisting scarlet strands. Peter pressed a glove to the ice. Fingers spread, he could cover the thing with one hand. He pulled his mother's drawing of mtDNA from his coat pocket and took off his gloves to unfold it, ignoring the immediate throbbing of his hands in the frigid air. He studied the sketch, peering now and again at the red ring under the ice. It couldn't be a coincidence. Was this what she was looking for? Had she put the thing here? Why?

Peter sat down on the sled and put a hand out to pat Sasha absently. She was having trouble settling down.

The dog paced a few restless circles and then started darting around making snuffling noises.

What was the matter with her? Peter unclipped her from the sled but kept a tight grip on a harness strap. And then he realized that he was hearing something. A high-pitched sound, like whistling, but with a purer tone. The wind, maybe. He listened again. It was almost like singing. Or wailing.

It was then that he remembered the polar bear. A shot of fear ricocheted around Peter's body. Did bears wail? Heart thumping, his mind ran through his father's advice: move slowly, stay far away from any cubs, and . . . and try to look big, something like that. He took his pack from the sled and put it on with some effort: He had stuffed half the contents of the equipment box into it, but he didn't have a single flare. It made him look bigger, anyway.

Sasha strained to run, but he held tight to her harness. Slowly, he let her pull him around one end of the ice wall to the other side, where the ground fell away in front of them into what looked like an empty lakebed, frozen and deep. The keening sound was getting louder. It didn't sound like any bear. More likely a wolf, he thought, calming down a little. Wolves, his father said, would stay away from him unless he got between a mother and her cubs.

He scanned the landscape in front of him. In the dim

light he could make out hummocks of ice here and there along the high edge of the slope, like clusters of white sails or giant shark teeth. He glanced from one to another, but the wailing was everywhere at once. Then the sound stopped, and the echoes fell silent.

There were a few moments in which nothing happened, but Sasha was still pulling hard. Peter let her pull him forward, just a step, and then the noise started up again, an arrow of sound that bounced around the frozen bowl in front of him. But this time he had a better sense of where it was coming from. Somewhere close.

EIGHTEEN

THEA

Thea's eyes were locked onto the slab of ice. Perhaps it had been a shadow moving, or an animal. She stood rooted to the ground and watched. Gru was mercifully silent. A dog's muzzle appeared, followed by its head and front legs—not Chikchu, but not far off either. And behind the dog was a boy.

He stood within shadow, and Thea had trouble seeing him at first. He was about her height, she thought, with rounded cheeks and curly hair the color of straw. It had never occurred to her that hair might come in different colors.

She looked back to the dog. She trusted animals implicitly, or wanted to, but she knew that dogs had been no friends to her people in the old world. The hunters had used them to root out hiding families, children in trees. She heard Meriwether's voice in her head, the one he used when he wanted to be dramatic. "The ancients hid well. But the hunters quickly discovered that their dogs could find them." She shivered.

Without warning, Gru started keening again, even louder now. Thea looked at her, followed the Chikchu's gaze to the boy and the huge wedge of ice he leaned against. She wasn't sounding an alarm, she realized. Gru was screaming for this boy. For him to come to them.

Fear drenched her in the moment it took to grasp what was happening. "Quiet!" Thea whispered, jerking Gru's harness roughly. "Stop that!"

Gru didn't spare her a glance. She was intent on the boy, who was looking off in the other direction, scanning the horizon, no doubt, for whatever was making such an awful racket. The sound was everywhere, echoing up to the sky, slipping off the slabs of ice that emerged here and there from the ground.

His dog was straining away from him now, but the boy held the animal by a collar with both hands. Who knew how many others might be near? Gru's wailing intensified so that Thea had to cover her ears with her hands.

Don't shout at her, she told herself, it will only make things worse.

She pulled with all her might on Gru's harness, but the Chikchu had planted her feet and could not be moved. Thea tried pressing hard on the dog's eyes, tried pinching her ears, but Gru would not be distracted. Thea couldn't look at the boy again, he might be turning, seeing them even now. She tore off one glove and raked her fingernails across Gru's sensitive muzzle. She knew from dressing pack-fight wounds that this hurt very much. Gru broke off for a second, let out a long growl of warning, and nipped Thea's hand. Hard. Then she growled again, longer and lower, took a few steps away from Thea, toward the edge of the steep slope, and set up a keening so loud it took Thea's breath away.

She could run for the tunnel. But what if the boy followed her? And what if he didn't? How could she leave Mattias helpless in the face of whatever this boy might do to him? Thea looked toward Mattias below. The sky was brighter now; it was nearly first light. Dawn.

Her hand ached, and she stuffed it quickly back into her glove. She had been fighting with Gru, with her mother's companion. Mattias would soon be lifeless on the ice, she was about to be discovered by the people of the wider world, and she had been clawing at a Chikchu.

Her feet stayed where they were. She turned away from Gru, away from Mattias, away from the slab of ice and the boy whose eyes would be on her any moment, and looked toward the glow and the warmth that had begun to break free of the horizon. The sun: She could feel it reaching for her, shedding rose and orange light all around her. Soon it would be right in front of her. She closed her eyes. She would not allow herself to look.

NINETEEN

PETER

The first thing he saw was an old-fashioned-looking sled, heaped with furs. It wasn't hitched to a team, but a gray dog stood nearby it. And holding the harness reins was a girl in a white fur with thick black curls falling almost to her waist. She was looking away from him, up at the sky.

They didn't seem quite real. There was something about the sled's curled runners, the girl's long hair, and the pile of furs that said to Peter, "This is all in your mind." But then Sasha began to run toward them, and Peter stumbled alongside, still holding on to her collar.

The dog dragged him right up to the girl. She was very real. Up close, she looked upset, with wet eyes and red blotches on her pale cheeks. He couldn't see much more of her, because she was covered from neck to foot in a somewhat dirty fur jumpsuit.

Sasha looked up at the girl. The wailing sound, which had been getting steadily louder, stopped abruptly as the big gray dog beside her swung its head to look at them.

The girl looked at Peter, at the same time extending a gloved hand for Sasha's inspection. She had definitely been crying.

"I am Thea," she said, her voice coarse. "I need your help."

"Peter," he stammered. To find anyone out here was unlikely enough, but a girl his age wrapped in fur?

"Peter," the girl repeated. Except that she said "Pita," like his mother.

"Are you from England?" Peter asked. "I thought we were the only people around here. Where is your camp?"

"No time for that," Thea said. "My friend is trapped." She pointed down the slope.

Peter followed her finger to where he could make out figures on the lakebed below them. Dogs. And a person. Without another word, the girl stepped on the back of her sled and flew down the steep slope, her dog running at her side.

His pack bouncing hard against his back, Peter ran back to his sled and pointed it down the slope just as the girl had. But then he lost his nerve and walked down, lowering the sled in front of him and scooting on his backside where the incline was too steep to walk. Sasha tried to stay with him, skidding frequently, as Peter kept his eyes on the girl and tried not to think about how he would get up to the top again.

When he caught up with her—Thea, she had said her name was—Peter gasped. The boy at their feet had been half-swallowed by the ice.

"His name is Mattias," Thea said, barely composed. "I'm afraid he's near death."

Peter nodded. The boy was unmoving and very pale, his eyes closed, his lips and eyelids blue. Was he alive?

The boy's torso emerged from a narrow crack in the ice. A white dog was stretched out alongside him, supporting his upper back and shoulders, and another, mostly black, had arranged itself against his chest so that his head seemed to emerge from a ring of black and white fur. The dogs were trying to warm him.

The girl said, "We won't be able to lift him without help. What have you brought?" She motioned to the knapsack on Peter's back. He'd forgotten he was wearing it.

He slipped the knapsack off and the two of them fell on it.

"What is this?" Thea asked frequently, holding up one object and then another. She didn't recognize an ordinary flashlight?

"Wait a minute!" Peter cried, seeing his hard-weather pod in the bottom of the bag. They could erect it around the boy's head and shoulders, but they would have to cut a hole in the bottom of the thing first. He looked back to the boy. Mattias.

"It won't get him out of there," he told Thea, "but it's worth the time. It has a heating element."

Tears streamed down Thea's cheeks. She nodded.

Peter tore the pod from its small sack, allowing it to spring open to its full size. Thea leaned away from it for a moment, as if she feared something might be about to leap out of the tiny tent.

Flipping the pod over, Peter felt for his knife in the front of his sack. He had never used it before.

"Hold it just like that," he said to Thea, stretching the underside of the pod with his hands until it was taut and smooth. She grasped the slick material and pulled it tight with a strength that surprised him. She looked about to fall apart.

With a gesture that suggested a good deal more confidence than he felt, Peter slashed a sizable "X" across the bottom of the pod. Then, taking a moment to fold the knife and toss it back into his sack, he felt along the pod's seams until he found the all the heaters: sealed packets of liquid chemical, divided by what felt like plastic Popsicle sticks. Peter used two hands to break the thin pieces of plastic. He could feel the heat through his gloves as the fluids washed together inside the pod's lining.

At a signal from Thea, the dogs moved away from Mattias and Peter covered him with the tiny tent, screwing the plastic anchors into the ice around him.

Thea was rooting through everything in Peter's sled now, opening the little bags strapped to the either side of the running board.

"What are these?" She held up the hand warmers he kept stashed there.

"Chemical warmers," he answered. "Like the ones heating the pod."

Thea's face lit up. "If we can wedge these alongside his legs, we could melt some of the ice around him. We might be able to pull him free."

It was a good idea. "They get really hot," Peter warned. "They're meant to be held with gloves."

"He's wearing a fur. He won't be burned."

Peter showed Thea how to break the plastic separators and they activated all but two of the warmers. Thea shoved them into deep pockets, in the legs of her fur, that had been invisible to him. She had a surprising amount of trouble with the pod's zipper, and accepted Peter's help with it before crawling inside.

Her three dogs kept watch over the end of the pod,

waiting for Thea to come out again. Sasha stayed close to Peter. He leaned against her, realizing that he was shaking. He didn't want to be here, where a boy might be about to die.

A few minutes later, Thea backed out of the pod and Peter zipped it closed behind her.

She was flushed. "Now we wait," she said. "Do you have anything that will help us to pull him out? We must lift him nearly straight up. The warmers may give us a bit of room, but the crevice is nearly vertical, and he's badly stuck."

Peter looked around at the things they had strewn around them in their panic. Nothing. They would just have to hope that the ice around him had loosened enough to let the two of them pull him out. It would help if the boy woke up.

"What happened?" he asked.

Thea looked up toward the top of the long slope and pointed to a line of small glaciers that looked like white sheets hanging from an invisible line.

"He slipped." Thea started crying again.

She stopped after a minute. The sun was up now, and she kept glancing up, shading her eyes with one hand. Peter offered her his goggles, but she just looked at them and shook her head.

Five long minutes later, they removed the small tent from around Mattias. Peter bent to support him under one shoulder while Thea took the other. They counted to three and tried to lift, but Peter knew in the first moment that the ice wouldn't give him up so easily.

"I'm going for help," Peter said. "My parents aren't far."

"No!" Thea shouted. "No. Don't go. Please, let's try one more time. Please."

If only the dogs could help, he thought. They were strong and certainly willing. The four of them stood together in a line now, watching solemnly.

"Wait a minute," Peter said. "Let's harness the dogs."

"Why? The dogs can't pull straight up, and he won't come free any other way. He is buried too deeply. They might tear him in half."

Peter reached for his sled, grasping the high backbar. "We can use this to make a pulley."

Thea nodded quickly. "Hurry. If the melted ice freezes around him again—"

Peter drew his sled up until the backbar was almost directly above Mattias's head and shoulders. Thea had somehow harnessed the dogs already, Sasha included. They lifted the harness strap over the sled's backbar and tied it as well as they could under Mattias's arms. Peter hoped he remembered the loop Jonas had taught him. Then they squatted to reposition themselves around Mattias, ready to try again.

"At three, then," said Thea. "One . . . two . . ."

Peter forgot to call out to Sasha, but all four dogs took off together on three, straining with incredible force while he and Thea struggled to stand.

Mattias came up all at once, Peter and Thea staggering under his weight until they reached Thea's sled, where they managed to lay him down on a bed of fur that Thea must have stretched out there. She began to strap him in quickly.

Peter fumbled to help, unable to suppress his questions any longer.

"Where are you going now?" he asked, patting the fur that Thea used to cover Mattias. "Are you camped close to here?"

Thea just shook her head as she attached her dogs to her sled. Peter harnessed Sasha to his own sled, hoping fervently that the dog could pull it up the icy slope while he climbed behind her.

Thea checked the straps around Mattias while Peter threw his equipment back onto his sled and tried to secure it. Mattias could still die; he wouldn't ask questions now. He walked up to Thea with the last two warmers.

She shook her head. "You may need them yourself."

Peter quickly squeezed them, breaking the starters, and tucked the warmers into the furs with Mattias. Thea nodded her thanks. Peter hoped she wasn't going to start crying again.

Thea stood behind her sled and gave the dogs a short command he didn't recognize. They began strongly, the three dogs pulling well, and a few moments later Peter and Sasha started up the hill behind them, Peter struggling a little to keep up but immensely relieved that his sled was moving at all with only Sasha to pull it.

Then, quickly, Thea's team slowed. She climbed up to her dogs, feeling their feet and ears, and swearing softly. She swore like his mother, too. Definitely English, he thought.

"Ham and Peg are half-frozen," she said, "lying all that time on the ice." Still talking, she began to cry. "Why didn't I think to put furs under them?"

"Frostbite?"

"I don't know that word. They are dangerously cold."

"But how? Aren't they, you know, snow dogs? Sasha never gets cold."

Thea stopped crying. "They aren't used to it—they sleep on sand, and their coats must have thinned. . . ." Her expression hardened. "I have to bring Mattias down a steep pathway, and they won't be much help. I have to ask you to come with us."

Peter nodded slowly, wondering for the first time how much time had passed since he left camp.

Thea harnessed Sasha alongside her dogs while Peter took his water, his flashlight, and a few other things from his sled and stowed them in his bag. With Sasha and the big gray dog pulling hard, Thea's sled kept moving while Thea and Peter climbed behind it.

Neither of them spoke, each focusing on the steep hill in front of them. They rested every few minutes at Thea's signal. At their second rest, Peter remembered the chocolate eggs in his pocket. He unwrapped four and passed two of them to Thea without a word. Although she looked none too eager to eat them, she put one into her mouth. In a few moments her eyebrows rose slightly and she gave him a small smile. He passed her two more and drank from his canteen, watching her raise what looked like an old cloth sack to her lips.

They continued on like this, breathing hard, making a little progress at a time and wasting no energy on words. Two of Thea's dogs, the white one and the black-and-white one, walked oddly—as if they were suddenly old—but with help from Sasha and the big gray dog, the sled was moving steadily.

At the top of the hill, they watered the dogs. Peter watched Thea pour water from her cloth sack into a shallow trough carved into the front of her sled.

"That's cool, a built-in water dish," Peter said. "And I thought my dad was the only westerner who rode sleds around Greenland. What's yours made out of?" He looked at it more closely. It looked like gray plastic, but not exactly.

"The usual things, I suppose," Thea said, looking down. Then her head jerked up as if she had heard something.

"What?" Peter said, looking all around. "Don't scare me like that."

Thea rushed to Mattias and gave a yelp of joy.

"He's moved! He turned his head!"

Mattias was waking. Thea carefully dripped some water into his mouth, and then accepted another chocolate egg from Peter. She unwrapped it carefully, saving the foil in a pocket, then bit off one end and put it in Mattias's mouth.

"Don't move. I'm afraid you're hurt." Peter heard her say as she rearranged the warmers under the fur that wrapped him. "We . . . We are bringing you home now."

Mattias's gaze swept around him until it found Peter. His glance shot back to Thea for a moment before he lost consciousness again.

Peter looked around for a campsite, wondering how much farther they might have to go. But there was nothing to see, other than the snow and the crusted ground and a few high ridges of ice. "Which way?" he asked.

Thea's relief returned some of her color to her. She looked like a different person as she rooted around under Mattias for a few moments and then tossed Peter a fur from the pile beneath him.

"Put it on. It is colder where there is no sun."

TWENTY

THEA

Peter stood uncertainly before Thea, shifting his weight from one foot to the other. The fur she gave him was too short in the leg, but she could hardly let him descend the flooded tunnel wearing the thin shiny thing he had ventured out in. He was lucky to be wearing high boots. She hoped they were lined with something very warm.

Even as these thoughts passed through her mind, she was aware that they veiled darker ones. What was she doing? Leading a boy of the wider world to the only refuge her people had ever known. It was unthinkable.

But how else was she going to get Mattias home?

She looked at Peter again. His companion trusted him—she had seen that right away. And this boy, of course, had had no part in the annihilation of her people in the old world. But his forebears may have. Their blood might flow in his veins.

Even half-conscious, Mattias had seemed to speak his vehement disapproval before he slipped away again. Maybe he had somehow stirred himself just to warn her. But with the water that still flowed down the tunnel's path, she, Gru, and the injured Chikchu could never stop the sleigh from hurtling down the passageway as quickly as the water blower had. A quick shudder went through her. Even with Peter's help, the sleigh could slip out of control.

She had no choice.

She set aside every thought but Mattias's survival.

"Are you all right?" Peter was looking at her anxiously.

"Certainly. I'm considering the best way down."

"A camp *inside* a glacier," Peter said, shaking his head while he rooted around in his bag. "I can't believe my father never told me about this. He'll be dying to see it."

Thea fought down a sense of panic.

Peter went on with his rummaging. "I have an idea." His hand came out of the bag. On his palm rested a thick shining loop with a sharply ridged protrusion about the length of her finger. It looked dangerous, and she recoiled.

"It's a screw." He looked at her strangely. "We can use it as an anchor. We could tie a rope to this and attach the other end to the sled. In case one of us, you know, slips."

When Thea didn't respond, he hesitated. "You know what a rope is, don't you?"

"Yes, I am familiar with rope," Thea said, trying to sound reproving but hearing herself as desperate. A rope leading into the tunnel was as good as an invitation to anyone passing this way.

Think of nothing but Mattias! Peter's plan made sense. She nodded.

They screwed the cold loop into the ice as well as they could, taking turns at it because they had to remove their gloves to grasp the thing and their hands numbed quickly. When it was secure, Peter brought out the rope and tied it to the loop. Thea tied the other end of the rope to her sleigh. It was not nearly long enough to reach to the bottom, Thea thought, but it would help.

"Wow," Peter said, probing the tunnel entrance with his flashlight. "You guys dug this out yourselves?"

Thea pretended not to hear as she harnessed the dogs to the back of the sleigh. She didn't trust herself to speak. She took one harness loop for herself and handed one to Peter. With Peg and Ham hurt, they would have to bear much of the sleigh's weight themselves.

They mounted Peter's flashlight to the front of the sleigh with a cord so that it cast a dim light ahead of them. Thea checked the sleigh straps one more time to make sure Mattias was tightly held.

"Brace yourself," she said. She gently pushed the sleigh into the steep passage until its weight pulled the traces taut. The dogs fanned themselves out to support it, Peter and Thea behind them.

Then Thea spoke to the Chikchu and they started off as one, leaning heavily on their front paws to restrain the sleigh, which threatened to hurtle down the tunnel. The four dogs inched down the passage, unused to the sight and the weight of the sleigh in front of them.

The tunnel seemed much steeper going down. Thea and Peter each had a harness strap wrapped tightly around a forearm, and they hugged the walls in an effort to avoid the worst of the water that flowed past them. The flashlight cast a weak glow over the ground in front of them, but failed to illuminate the murals on the walls. Thea took a moment to feel grateful for that bit of luck, and for the fact that the work of finding footholds left little time for questions.

It was cold. At the steepest parts, they gave up walking and scooted along the tunnel floor in a sitting position, bracing themselves with their heels. This meant sitting in the icy stream that still rushed down the tunnel; their furs kept them dry, but couldn't entirely protect them from the chill.

"Is it, uh, usually like this?" Peter asked. He was breathing hard. "With the water?"

"No," Thea said fiercely, so that he wouldn't ask more. She couldn't help feeling a bit mean.

The dogs, walking in the stream of water that flowed over the icy floor, slipped from time to time, but they all kept their harness lines taut and took on as much of the sleigh's weight as they could manage. Thea praised them every few minutes, and Peter began to do the same, remembering her Chikchus' names and earnestly telling them that they were something called "real troupers." She was coming to like him.

They traveled the length of the rope and then rested, rubbing their sore wrists while the sleigh was still anchored by the screw at the top of the passage. They drank water and allowed themselves three chocolates each.

Thea checked on Mattias while Peter watered the dogs. She watched with interest from where she knelt next to the sleigh as Peter patted each of the animals in turn, speaking softly.

"You are quite good with them," she said.

Peter smiled. "That's what my mother says."

"Your mother is right." Thea reached into a fold of fur at the back of her sleigh, straightening up again with the lightglobe in her hands. "We need more light," she said, glancing at Peter's flashlight, which had begun to flicker.

He winced. "The batteries."

Thea suspended her lightglobe by its woven strap. She spun the globe's small knob and it blazed to life with a bright green light.

Peter's eyes widened.

"It's fueled by oxygen," Thea said quietly. "The knob controls the flow. I promise to answer the rest of your questions when we get to . . . the bottom."

Peter nodded.

It was time to untie the rope. Thea found two good footholds and managed to hold the sleigh with the dogs' help while Peter untied their lifeline. Then he grasped his harness loop again and looked at her.

"Ready."

They were exhausted, and their progress was more painful now. It was more and more difficult to find footholds that would support the sleigh's weight. Their feet slipped continually, and their hands were of little use, as they had to keep their grips on the harness loops.

Peter interrupted their concentrated silence. "We need to rest."

"How?" Thea's arm muscles were trembling.

"I've been thinking," Peter said. "The tunnel isn't very wide. If we can get the sled to go sideways, maybe we can wedge it across the passageway."

Thea was doubtful. It was too easy to lose control of the sleigh.

"We have to do something," Peter said. "My arms are about to give." His face was pinched and white in the green light.

She nodded. "It's worth trying."

They struggled to grip the sleigh's curled runners and managed to drive its head against the tunnel wall. Peter let the back of the sleigh slip in a slow arc until it came to rest against the opposite wall. It seemed to hold. Shaking with fear, Thea loosened her grip slowly, uncurling her fingers with effort. The sleigh stayed where it was. She let out a long breath, her arms and legs trembling.

They sat without speaking. Thea supposed that, like her, Peter was feeling the throbbing of his muscles and wondering how in the world he had come to be here. Thea summoned what was left of her reason to make a plan.

But she disliked the only plan her mind could manage. Disliked it very much. She didn't even know how to propose it.

"You're right," she started, looking at the ground in front of her. "We aren't in very good order, are we? I think it would help me if I could free my hands."

"Free your hands? How? You can't let go of the sled."

"I will tie myself to the sleigh," Thea said. "I'll loop the harness strap around me and then continue on. I think you should go back up. I'll be able to make my way down. It isn't so much farther."

"By yourself? You'll never make it! And tied to the sled . . ." He didn't finish the sentence.

Yes, she thought, if I slip I'll be dragged down after the sleigh and smashed to bits at the bottom. "There is no alternative," Thea said. "Mattias is my family. I must do what I can."

"Look," Peter said. "Let's leave him here and go down ourselves. Get help."

Thea shook her head. "There's no way to know whether the sleigh will hold that long. I'm not going down without him."

"Then let's get going," Peter said, strapping the harness loop around his midriff and tying it. "We're wasting time."

"No," Thea said, turning to face him for the first time. "This is more than I can ask of you. Mattias is a stranger to you, as am I."

"Do you really think I'm going to climb back up there while you two slide to your deaths? Let's go, I'm numb." Peter pulled the strap more tightly around him. The dogs all stood up at once, which somehow made his decision final.

When they had checked each other's knots, Thea and Peter edged the sleigh out of its resting place, making sure it didn't come loose all at once.

They advanced by inches and an eternity of held breaths until the ground began to level. Soon they could walk upright, and the water flow had slowed to a trickle. They freed themselves from the sleigh traces and held the lines loosely with their throbbing hands. Thea vowed that she would never again take the painless miracle of walking on two legs for granted.

Then the lantern threw its dim glow over the tunnel entrance. As Mattias had predicted, their crude entrance was almost completely sealed by ice. That was why the water flow had nearly stopped: there was no longer an air current to guide the water. She glanced around—where was the blower?

Fear coursed through her: What if the blower was on the other side? She stared at the wall of ice. A small hole remained of their opening, hardly big enough to put her fist through. She was trying to peer through it when she heard voices on the other side. Thea recognized one.

"Lucian, it's Thea! We're behind the wall!"

A woman's rough voice answered—Thea didn't recognize it. "Stand well back!" She and Peter pushed the sleigh back as hot water showered over them.

The new ice melted quickly, and soon an arm was thrust through the hole.

"Come," the rough voice said, "one at a time."

"No," Thea called, "we need more room. Mattias is hurt, strapped to the sleigh."

"Not much time," Thea heard Lucian say. Before what? She wondered.

Water shot through the hole in a steady stream, and it widened slowly until Thea shouted "Big enough!" Holding tightly to the front of the sleigh where Mattias still lay unconscious, she and Peter inched forward through a large warm puddle of water. Then they were crouching to step through the opening.

The arm was extended again, and Thea grasped it as she stepped through the hole, emerging to find herself gripping the strong hand of Mattias's grandmother, Dexna.

TWENTY-ONE

THEA

"She is her mother's daughter," said Dexna, holding fast to Thea as she looked her up and down. "Are you hurt anywhere?"

"I don't think so," Thea said slowly. Dexna—speaking? And with a forcefulness she could not have imagined.

Lucian stood beside Dexna, breathing hard with exertion. The handblower was on the ground beside him.

Before Thea could do or say anything else, Peter was struggling through the hole. Thea extended a hand to help him down. "Mattias would not be alive if Peter had not helped us. He has risked his own life for ours."

Lucian and Dexna stared at Peter for a long moment. Thea had no idea what they might do, but she certainly didn't expect Lucian's bow and Dexna's handshake.

"Hello," Peter said, then stared at the vast lake surrounded by thin-trunked trees. His mouth hung open. Through the trees, Thea could make out the forms of skaters flying along the Mainway on the way back to their workposts after their noontime meals. He would have a lot of questions.

Could it be possible that no one was going to start screaming at her? The moment Thea had so dreaded passed, and then the four of them were lowering the sleigh carefully to the ground. Mattias still slept.

"He fell," Thea said. "His legs were wedged into the ice. I didn't think we were going to be able to lift him . . ."

Dexna quickly loosened the straps and furs around Mattias and began feeling his limbs, lifting his eyelids, shifting his head gently in her hands. After a minute she gave a sharp nod and said, "No permanent harm done."

"Are you sure? He'll be himself again?" Thea submitted to a cursory examination, but then shook off Dexna's hands, forcing herself to speak more confidently than she felt.

"I'm fine. I must find Dolan to care for Ham and Peg—they've frozen their paws." She flipped down her skate blades, feeling Peter's eyes on her.

"You'd best come to the archive with us first," Dexna

said as she began to wrap Mattias in the furs again. She came across one of Peter's handwarmers and poked it experimentally. Thea was about to explain when Dexna shrugged and shoved it beneath a fur. Nothing appeared to surprise the woman.

"I'll send a messenger to your aunt Lana," Dexna went on. "I believe Dolan is at your chambers as well, along with Sela. You and Mattias were both missed at first light. They've been worried."

Dexna gestured Peter to her own sleigh, where Lucian was busy obscuring the blower with some empty cloth sacks. Peter was still gaping at the lake. He seemed interested in the empty fishing docks now, though the boats were all out of sight across the lake. She wondered just how strange all of this was to him.

"We'll have to wait a bit if we want to avoid a lot of attention on the backways," Lucian said.

Thea shook her head. "I can't wait. I have to get Dolan—I'll bring him to the archive." She turned to Peter. "You go with them. I'll be straight there." And before anyone could say another word, she skated off toward the Mainway.

Thea stumbled on her skates just before she reached the first pass, catching herself before she hit the hard ground of the Mainway. She needed rest. It was midday and full light, yet everything looked dim to her, even after her hours in the dark tunnel. All of the light had a greenish tinge to it, she realized. How had she never noticed it before?

She knew she had to decide what to say to Lana, but the ability to think logically escaped her. The best she could manage was one deep breath while she flipped up her skate blades before opening the door.

Lana stood near the greatroom basin with Sela. Their faces flooded with relief.

Dolan sat at the long table, a bowl of food in front of him. Seeing it, Thea had two realizations: One, she was almost as hungry as she was tired. And two, Dolan must be upset indeed. His plate was untouched.

Dolan rose to his feet. "Deceit, Thea? Deceit? I thought I knew you. You may consider your duties at the breeding grounds concluded. I will not put Chikchu lives into the hands of a person so unworthy of trust!"

He was almost shouting, which was a shock. She had never heard him raise his voice before, except to be heard over a pack fight. Too exhausted to cry, she stood just inside the door, shaking her head mutely.

Finally noticing the state of Thea's fur and the scratches on her hands, Dolan softened his tone. "Are you hurt? What happened to you up there? Thea, where is Mattias?"

Thea kept shaking her head. These were three of the most important people in her life. How could she tell them that she had risked Mattias, that she had almost lost him, so that she might have a glimpse of the wider world? And another thought crept in: Had Dolan said "up there"?

Sela grabbed her hands and forced Thea to meet her gaze. "Where is Mattias?"

Sela must fear the worst. "Mattias is safe," she managed. "He is with his grandmother at the archive."

Sela kissed Thea and flew out the door.

Thea felt herself sway a bit. She turned to Dolan. "Peg needs care, and Ham. They are at the archive too. Will you help me with them?"

Already starting for the dock door, Dolan said, "I have a team here, we'll take the backways. It will take a while longer arriving, but we'll have the proper equipment when we . . ."

"Dolan," Lana interrupted quietly. "Thea cannot go with you. Have sense."

Thea had every intention of going. She had to get to the archive. Peg was there, hurt. Mattias was in no condition to explain to everyone what had happened, and the boy Peter was surely bewildered beyond words. She had promised to see him back home.

She tried to frame a sentence in her mind, a place to start. She wanted Lana to know about the tunnel, and the murals. She wanted Lana to know that they were meant to rejoin the wider world. She wanted to explain about Mattias, to share the depths of that despair with someone who would truly understand, and to tell her about Peter, and what he and his dog had risked for them. She wanted to tell Lana about the stars, and the air, and the sun, and the vastness of the surface.

No time. She had to get back to Mattias, to Ham and Peg, to Peter. She tried to cross the greatroom behind Dolan, but her feet were taking tiny steps, as if she were a child again. Just as she felt herself falling, Thea was embraced from behind.

"I have you," Lana said. Thea's eyes closed against her will as Lana cradled her, easily holding her aloft in arms strengthened by a lifetime of nurturing.

TWENTY-TWO

PETER

Peter stared at the lake. How could Thea have left him here without telling him what was going on?

It was obvious the place was more than a camp. Peter had seen enough to know that before he was five steps out of the tunnel. His father had told him that there were such things as freshwater lakes deep inside the ice sheet—they were heated by magma, and gases that escaped through fissures in the earth. But Peter was pretty sure they didn't come equipped with docks or trees along the shore. Or benches under the trees.

The man and woman talked quietly together. Every few minutes the woman leaned over to touch Mattias's face or pat the furs around him. They had asked Peter to sit on another sled, one they must have brought with them, and now they seemed to have forgotten all about him. He kept one hand on Sasha.

The lake was vast and glimmering. He couldn't see the far side—the water just faded into darkness. Peter looked up and found that the ceiling, about ten feet above his head, was shedding a bright, faintly green light. How? He wondered if it had to do with the humming sound he heard.

The woman began to come toward him. Her fur was a little different from Thea's. It was open at the collar, and had loose sleeves that flapped at her wrists when she walked. She held a grayish cup out to him. "Water," she said. "Best thing after a journey."

He took it and drank. It tasted like water.

When she raised her hand to take the cup from him, one of her sleeves fell back, revealing something clasped to her arm. Something that was a shade of red he knew well. His heart began to pound. This place had something to do with the ring in the ice.

Something to do with his mother.

"Ready, then?" The woman smiled. "Lucian will escort you to the top of the passage."

"Now, you mean? But . . . won't I see Thea again?"

The woman looked surprised, and shook her head. "I'm afraid not."

"But . . . but how is it that you live here? Are there lots of other people? What are you doing down here?"

The woman looked him over slowly, from head to toe and back up to his face again. Then she sat down next to him. Her hair, twisted into a bun, was a silvery gray, but her skin was remarkably smooth. Something about her dark brown eyes, shaped like almonds, made him want to like her.

"We don't know each other, but I can feel goodness in you," she said. "And I am sorry, but I cannot answer your questions."

He absorbed that, trying not to be scared. She took one of his hands in hers. They felt cool and feathery.

"And I will ask you not to return here, though you may be curious about this place. I won't demand your word. We both know that I have asked, and perhaps that will be enough."

She didn't say it rudely. Peter got the sense she was trying not to hurt his feelings. He nodded, and then decided to take one last shot. "Can I ask one thing? You can say no."

She smiled again, and Peter noticed flecks of green in her eyes. "You may ask me a question."

"Can I see what's on your arm?" He nodded to her right hand.

Her expression changed—she was calculating something—and then her face relaxed again. "I can think of no reason why not," she said, and raised her sleeve to reveal a row of bracelets exactly like the one in the ice wall. Twisting bands, the color of blood.

He had no idea what showed on his face.

"Do these mean something to you?" Her tone was friendly, but it was obvious that the question was important to her.

"No—no, I've just never seen anything like them before. They're pretty. I mean, that's a nice color."

She nodded and dropped her arm. "I must see to my grandson now." She looked at him very closely, as if she were trying to memorize his face. "Good-bye, Peter."

Peter nodded and stood up. "Bye." He didn't know her name.

"What's that noise?" Peter asked the man—Lucian—when they were at the tunnel entrance.

"What noise?" Lucian looked around quickly.

"It sounds sort of like a heartbeat. Don't you hear it?"

The man looked relieved. "A heartbeat. How apt an analogy that is. Yes, I do hear it," he said. "But I am unaware of it for the most part."

It wasn't much of an answer. Lucian seemed to enjoy questions about as much as Thea and the old woman did.

Lucian waved Peter toward the tunnel. "Just push yourself through. I'll send your companion after you."

Peter climbed awkwardly into the tunnel. Without Thea's light, it was almost completely black. He heard Sasha somewhere near him. He tried to feel his way to her and hoped that he wasn't about to collide with Lucian.

The passage suddenly blazed around them—Lucian stood holding a round lamp like the one Thea had used. Peter squinted against the bright light.

Then Lucian was striding along ahead of him.

There was no longer any water on the tunnel floor, and the walking was relatively easy at first. But Lucian managed to stay well ahead of Peter, making it difficult to talk.

"Why are we in such a hurry?" Peter asked after a quick scurry that caught him up for a moment.

"I'd like to get back down before someone notices that hole in the wall," Lucian snapped. He was touchy.

"Oh," Peter said. "Is it like a secret back door or something?"

Lucian stopped walking and turned to him. "It is the only door."

"The only door," Peter repeated. Surely these people didn't live sealed up in ice.

"Yes." Lucian looked at him steadily. "Our people were hunted. Our ancestors created this land so that we might live in peace."

"But why? Where did you come from? You all sound like you're from England! Who would want to hurt you?"

Lucian walked with his eyes on his feet. "Our people were from England, originally. So were our pursuers: We fled to the cold world—to the place you know on the surface."

"You mean Greenland?"

Lucian looked at Peter searchingly. "It is your home, then?"

"No! I'm from New York. I'm just visiting—my dad is a scientist, he studies glaciers.

The tunnel was gradually getting steeper, and Peter leaned hard into his strides. Sasha stayed next to him. They walked in silence for a time. Drawings appeared on the passage walls: people, dogs, bundles of furs and other things on sleds. He hadn't noticed them on the way down—too busy trying to hang on to the sled.

"I just think that I could help you," Peter said after a while. "Or my parents could. My mother is English, too."

He was just looking for things to keep Lucian talking. But he had clearly said the wrong thing.

Lucian stopped and fixed him with a dark look.

205

"Forgive me if I am not comforted by the fact of an Englishwoman in Greenland. Some believe that we may have been followed here."

"But that's crazy," Peter said. "There are no people waiting up there for you! My mother isn't looking for you! She's a scientist!" But as he was speaking, three images flashed in the back of Peter's mind: the ring in the ice wall, the old woman's bracelets, and his mother's drawing of mitochondrial DNA.

"Is she?" Lucian asked. "What kind of scientist?"

The pieces were coming together too quickly. "What?"

"What kind of a scientist is your mother?"

"She's a biologist." A biologist who absentmindedly doodles pictures of jewelry from your secret world. A biologist who is looking for something. He heard her voice: *Find it for me, Gregory.* But his mom couldn't be any sort of hunter. That was impossible.

Lucian didn't say anything. He started walking again.

Peter could see his rope lying on the tunnel floor now, leading out of the passageway. He wished Lucian wouldn't walk so fast. "But . . . how do you breathe? All closed in down there?"

The tunnel was steep now, but Lucian didn't break his stride. "We draw our air from the surface, through tiny channels in the ice. I'm afraid I have no more time for questions."

They were at the top of the passage. Two words were written over the archway that led outside—"Hope lives"—but Lucian hardly gave them a glance as he stepped under them and into a light wind. The sun was high but clouded over.

"Can you find your way from here?" Lucian asked, glancing up.

"Yes," Peter said. He thought of his sled at the bottom of the steep hill. More climbing.

Lucian nodded. "I'm afraid I'll need that fur," he said.

Peter felt almost undressed in his coat. He had gotten used to the weight of the fur.

Lucian put his hands on Peter's shoulders and said, "Thank you for helping Thea bring Mattias back to us. And remember what I have told you."

"I will," Peter said. "And you're welcome."

Peter and Sasha began to walk down toward their sled. Peter looked back once and saw Lucian standing at the edge of the slope, watching them, but the second time he looked the man was gone.

When they had dragged the sled back to the top of the long hill, Peter saw that his hook and rope were gone, too. He turned and walked toward home slowly, Sasha pulling the sled and Peter walking behind it. His body had never been so tired, but his brain felt wide awake. Had he really just been to a place no one else knew existed? Why had these people been hunted? Was his own mother looking for them? Was his father?

By the time their camp came into view, it was hard for Peter to believe it was still the same day he'd left. As Sasha drew the sled up to the dogs' shelter, Peter's father came out of the blue tent, zipping his jacket. He looked upset.

"Sorry, I know it's late," Peter started. "But I had all of my emergency equipment, in case anything came up."

"Good," his father said. He was distracted. "Peter, I came out here because I want you to be prepared. Your mother is having a bad patch."

Peter thought of their living room at home, of the chair she always propped her body in during her "headaches" while her mind went someplace else.

"Sometimes these things go quickly, Peter. She may be herself in the morning."

That had happened. Once. "Is she talking?" Peter asked.

His father looked at the ground. "No, she isn't."

He didn't want to go inside the tent. He unharnessed Sasha, gave her some water, and shook food into a dish for her. He stowed the sled.

His father waited. "Ready?"

They went in together. Jonas was setting the table, and he gave Peter a smile and a wave, but looked uncomfortable for the first time since Peter had known him. The curtain was drawn across the foot of Peter's parents' bed.

"Come on," his father said gently, ducking behind it.

His mother was lying in bed, leaning against all four of the pillows with her eyes closed, and yet clearly not asleep. Peter looked around for her red notebook, but it was nowhere in sight. The notebook was to blame for this. He had seen it sucking the life out of her day after day.

His father sat on the edge of the bed, and Peter stood next to him. She didn't acknowledge either of them.

"Hi, Mom," Peter said. There was no response. His father was rubbing her hand, as if her problem might be a simple lack of circulation.

Peter wanted to tell them everything: about his visions, and Thea and Mattias and the place they came from. He wanted to hand over all of it, to let them figure out the causes and the effects and the right answers. His sudden desire to be free of it all sat like a ball stuck at the base of his throat.

"We'll get through this one, too, Pete," his father said.

Peter nodded. There was nothing worse than this.

His father put his mother's hand back on the bed and looked at Peter. "You must be hungry. Let's eat."

Jonas had heated four frozen chicken pot pies for lunch. Peter didn't recognize his hunger as hunger, but he finished his food quickly, still thinking of the red notebook. Tomorrow he would find it, and destroy it.

His father pushed the extra pie across the table to him,

and Peter mechanically crushed its crust roof with his spoon.

Jonas smiled. "Hard work this morning, huh? Out looking for the Second Volkswagen Road?"

The pot pie steamed on Peter's plate like the smoking remains of a building collapse. "Something like that," he said.

TWENTY-THREE

THEA

When Thea woke sometime after last light, so many thoughts crowded her head that she squeezed her eyes closed and tried to return to the blissful mindlessness of sleep. It was no use—her mind raced among Mattias, the tunnel, Peg and Ham, the boy Peter, the warmth of the sun on her face. And although she was just barely conscious of it, a howling hunger had settled over her.

She began one of Lana's breathing exercises and tried to remember the vastness of the night sky. What glory it had been to see the star patterns reveal themselves one by one, welcoming her!

Her eyes opened. Lana's painted stars glowed just over-head. She finally had her answers, she realized. She understood now why she had been made to learn the star patterns, along with the principles of navigating a ship, and the fact that an animal called a pig is bigger than one called a cat. Like every generation before her, she was being prepared to live in the world—the wider world. Had no one else put these things together? When had the purpose of all this teaching been lost?

She sat up carefully and noticed that she was dressed in a fresh tunic and leggings. A thin fur wrap had been left at the foot of her bed, and her bracelets were stacked neatly on her trunk. She stepped down from the bed and reached for the wrap, hoping that the whole first line wasn't waiting for her in the greatroom.

She ventured from her sleeping chamber slowly, braced by the chill of the greatroom and immeasurably cheered to see her aunt sitting at the long table, alone. Lana was crushing dried herbs with a tiny mortar and pestle.

She gave Thea a broad smile. "Hungry?"

"Mattias," Thea started, "is he—"

"Mattias sleeps. And Dexna has promised me that he will be himself again."

Thea felt a rush of joy. Mattias would be all right, and for a few moments nothing else mattered. She sat slowly, pulling the warm wrap around her shoulders. Even this small movement caused her body to ache in several places. She looked at her aunt carefully as Lana stood and went to the counter, returning with a small platter. Wasn't she upset?

The salad was Thea's favorite, smoked fish with bitterest greens, and Lana had saved a generous length of the evening bread. Forgetting everything else, Thea began to eat. The salty fish on a crunchy heel of bread was impossibly good.

Lana had taken up her place before the herbs again. As Thea ate, she began to wonder why her aunt asked her no questions. When her plate was clean, she sat back.

"Is Peg here?" she asked carefully.

"Peg will be fine, too. She is recovering at the archive with Ham. Dexna was here to see you a short while ago."

"Lana, Dexna can speak!"

Lana looked up quickly, no surprise on her face. "Yes," she said quietly, "though for a long time she has chosen not to."

"But why?"

Lana rubbed the end of the pestle with her thumb. "The answer to that question is tangled among many others. Dexna's choice to be silent is her way of reminding us—some of us—of another voice that was silenced."

"Whose?"

"For the rest of the answers, you must wait a little

while. And while we are on the topic of secrets, Thea, I am one of very few who know where you and Mattias have been. We must leave it that way for now."

"Leave it that way? But the tunnel, the murals—Lana, it's all wrong, what we think. Our foremothers never meant for us to remain here, and Rowen must be told, everyone must know . . ."

Lana interrupted her gently. "Rowen knows of the passage, Thea. She has known of it for a long time."

"She knows? She cannot know. She said there was no passage to . . ." She wished her mind could work more quickly. "She lied, then, at the council meeting, when she said there was no way to the surface."

"Yes," Lana said. "There is a great deal for us to tell each other, Thea."

"What are you saying?" Thea asked plaintively. "Have you all seen the surface then? Why won't you simply tell me?"

"I have not seen it." Lana rose to take the kettle from the fire. "And I want to hear everything. For the rest, well, you have very little time left to wait." She set a cup of hot, sweet ricewater in front of Thea, cradling one for herself.

Thea took a long drink. What was the meaning of all this? She had awakened believing that she was going to enlighten the citizens of Gracehope, and instead she was the one looking for answers.

"There is a story I want to tell you, Thea, while we still have time."

Still have time? Thea thought. Where are we going?

"When you were very small, just starting to skate—you couldn't have been more than two years old—you became very attached to a toy ricewater pot that had been floating among the children of the old quarter for some time. It was plain-looking, the lid had been lost and the decoration rubbed off. For a month, you carried it around with you everywhere."

"I don't remember it."

"I would be very surprised if you did." Lana reached out and smoothed Thea's hair. "One day, you were playing with the pot at the gardens while I worked, and you somehow wedged two round stones into the bottom of it. You handed the pot to me, wanting the stones out. And I tried, but the stones simply couldn't be moved. I still wonder that you got them into it in the first place."

Lana gestured to Thea's cup, and she obediently drained the last of her ricewater.

"You were very frustrated," Lana continued, "and so I put the pot aside and distracted you with something else. The next day, I gave it back to you, but you became enraged about the stones all over again, demanding that they come out. Again I put the pot away, thinking that you would eventually forget about the stones and enjoy the pot as you had before.

215

"But you never could forget. Every time I gave you the pot, you checked to see if the stones had gone, and you became angry again. Finally I passed the thing on to another line. It brought you nothing but frustration and grief."

Lana paused. "Do you have any idea why I am telling you this story, Thea?"

Thea thought for a moment. Her toes had begun to tingle pleasantly with warmth.

"Something to do with stubbornness?" she asked. The warmth was traveling up her legs.

"That's one way to put it. My point is this: Once you found fault with the ricewater pot, you couldn't enjoy it at all. It became a source of misery because it was no longer exactly as you wanted it to be. But every person has to learn to accept what has happened in the past. Without bitterness. Or there is no point in continuing with life. I want you to keep this in mind tomorrow."

"Why? What happens tomorrow?" The warmth had reached her fingertips, the back of her neck, her eyelids. She was very sleepy. She realized with a start that her ricewater had been more than ricewater. That's why it was so sweet, she thought. But she was too tired to be upset about it.

Lana smiled, giving Thea's arm a light squeeze. "I'll walk you back to bed. Nothing more will happen tonight."

One thing pressed on Thea more than the others. As she allowed her aunt to lead her back to her sleeping chamber, she asked, "Will you see Dolan tonight?"

Lana nodded. "I expect I will. He's been here to see about you several times already."

"Will you apologize for me? I don't think I managed to."

Lana smiled. "Don't worry about Dolan. It's just that he loves you, and he doesn't understand his own line in some ways. He's been hurt so badly . . ." She trailed off.

Another hint. Thea would demand full explanations when she had the energy, but for the moment she was content to climb back into bed. It was still warm.

TWENTY-FOUR

PETER

In the morning, his dad said Peter's mother was sleeping, but in fact she was more half-asleep, stirring and murmuring when Peter went in to ask if she felt hungry. Her sounds were like words that she couldn't quite pronounce, or maybe she was saying them in a dream.

His dad made pancakes. They usually just had cold cereal for breakfast, with some fresh bread from the bread-maker. Peter wondered if the pancakes were to tempt his mother out of bed, or if they were supposed to cheer Peter up. Maybe his father just wanted something to do. He made about four times as many as they could eat.

It was awkward trying to act normal. Jonas raved about the pancakes for a full five minutes. Peter watched the muscles of his father's jaw jump and twitch. Why couldn't they just *talk* about it? Let's say it: Mom is in bad shape. How will we get through it this time? But the heaviness in his throat stopped him. Instead, he clapped loudly for Jonas, who managed to eat sixteen pancakes.

"I'll do the dishes," Peter said as Jonas stepped into his boots.

"Thanks, Pete." His dad rested a hand on Peter's head. "If you can clear me a syrup-free space, I think I'll work here for a while."

That was the last thing Peter wanted. "You don't have to do that, Dad. Don't you need your computers?"

Dr. Solemn hesitated. His jaw twitched. "Are you okay here, alone?"

"I'm fine," Peter said. In fact, he had a headache. "And anyway, you're only fifty feet away."

"I have to go take some readings later. If you want I can have Jonas stay—"

"Dad, I'm fine. What's Jonas going to do around here? I'll make sandwiches for lunch, and then both of you can go."

It was a great relief when his father finally went out the door. Peter's headache was getting worse, and he wanted to look for his mother's red notebook.

He pulled back his parents' curtain. His mom seemed to be sleeping for real now. Peter put his hand on her forehead, the way she always did for him. "Mom," he said quietly. But she was somewhere else.

He looked around. The red notebook wasn't on the bed, or the shelf. He opened the drawers under the bed and rifled through them. Two of them held nothing but clothes and the third was full of his mothers' old catalogs and magazines—she said they were the only things that could put her to sleep at night; everything else was too absorbing and kept her awake.

He pulled each one out and threw it on the floor. The notebook was nowhere. Head pounding, he began shoving the magazines and catalogs back into the drawer. The top of a writing pad stuck out of one—white paper, green lines, and a thin cardboard back. He slipped it out.

On the paper, his mother had drawn trees. Long, thin trees with big leaves that grew around the edge of a lake. There was no doubt in his mind that he was looking at Thea's trees, Thea's lake.

Peter's head swam for a moment, but his thinking was clear. He would return to the tunnel. And this time he wouldn't leave without answers.

He went into the kitchen, made a bowl of tuna fish for

his dad and Jonas, and set it on the table with a bag of thawed bread and a box of cookies. He washed the breakfast dishes.

Peter put a new rope and hook into his knapsack along with a small tarpaulin. He knew his coat wasn't as waterproof as the fur Thea had given him, and he thought he might sit on the tarp and scoot down the tunnel if he had to.

He went to the cargo line and took a handful of dried peaches, some ham, and two frozen rolls. He pushed all of it together into a small plastic bag. His headache was raging, and he seemed to be limited to one thought at a time. He put the plastic bag into his knapsack. He filled a canteen with water. Then he kissed his mother on the forehead and went to get Sasha.

At the dogs' house, he grabbed the lightest sled and as many treats for Sasha as he could stuff into one coat pocket.

Then, ignoring the throbbing of his head, Peter stepped onto the sled and they set off to the west.

Five minutes later, Peter was trembling and drenched with sweat. He could just see the ice wall, a bump among other bumps on the horizon. As he looked at it, a fluttering started at the edges of his vision.

Aha! He thought. You're back.

He was so hot. He unzipped his jacket. It didn't seem to help.

He stepped off the sled, stumbling away from it before falling to his knees in the snow. Isn't that funny, he thought to himself as he lay down, it isn't even cold.

He gazed up at the sky, where he could make out stars, though part of him knew that couldn't be right. It was daytime! The stars expanded, pinpricks of light growing into small orbs that blazed in a friendly way against the sky. And then all at once the world went black, which came as a relief, like someone shutting the lights off when you are too tired to do it yourself.

Peter knew nothing when Sasha, whimpering and still dragging the sled, lay down alongside him, raised her head, and began to call for help.

TWENTY-FIVE

THEA

When she woke again, Lana was gone. It was Sela who sat at the greatroom table.

"Feeling rested?" she asked brightly. "Dolan is expecting you at the breeding grounds this afternoon."

"He is?" Dolan wasn't going to banish her from the grounds after all! "Sela . . ." Thea couldn't bear to meet her eyes. "It's my fault, everything. Mattias didn't want to go to the surface, not after the tunnel started flooding. But I wouldn't turn back, and Mattias almost died."

Sela got up from the table and stood before Thea, lifting her chin with two fingers. "Mattias is fine. Or he will be, shortly. I won't say what the two of you did was particularly intelligent. But no one is angry, not yet anyway. You have cured a kind of paralysis, Thea, suffered by everyone in Gracehope, and by the first bloodline in particular. But I can't say more, because I promised Mattias that you would both hear the story at the same time, and now I've gone and told you half of it already. But first, wash, and eat. If I bring you around dirty and starved Lana won't speak to me for a sevennight. Now hurry."

Thea needed no urging. But halfway to the wash chamber she turned to Sela and said, "It was you who left me the map, wasn't it Sela?"

Sela shook her head. "The map wasn't mine to give."

The backways were nearly empty, and Thea was silent as their sleigh sped along. She expected Sela to take the pass to the archive, but they flew right past it. Not a minute later, the dogs drew them up into one of the sleigh docks beside the lake path.

"Here we are," Sela said.

Thea looked around. The place wasn't busy. The fishing boats were still out on the water, and the two long docks were deserted.

"Why are we here?" Thea asked. "Where is Mattias?"

"Mattias is at the archive," Sela said. "He is in no condition to skate."

"But you said we were going to hear the story together."

"I said you would hear the story at the same time. Mattias will hear it from his grandmother at the archive. And you will hear it here."

"From you?"

"From Lucian."

Thea stiffened. "Lucian? But why?"

Sela took one of Thea's wrists and squeezed it. "Because he asked that it be him." She glanced over Thea's shoulder. "Here he is now."

Thea turned in time to see Lucian coast the last few yards to the lake path. He was tall and lean, and skated with a grace that took her by surprise. She always thought of him hunched over a desk and scowling. He came to a sharp stop in front of them and nodded once.

"How are you, Thea?" His eyes were on the ground, but there was the usual intensity to his voice.

She straightened her shoulders. "Fine, thank you."

"Well, I'll be leaving you to it, I suppose." Sela rubbed her hands together for a moment and then let them drop to her sides. "Thea, don't forget that you're wanted at the breeding grounds this afternoon."

"I remember," Thea said.

"Lucian—" Sela started, but then she embraced him and walked off to her sleigh without looking back.

Thea stared after her. She had never seen Sela at a loss for words.

"Shall we walk?" Lucian gestured to the lake path that wound away from the docks under the trees.

"Of course." Thea inclined her head. She wouldn't embarrass herself by jumping in with a lot of questions.

"I'll begin at the beginning," Lucian said, and they set off on the path.

"Some twenty years ago, a group of our young engineers began to study the possibility of enlarging our world. They were not interested, at first, in the planet's surface. They considered it nothing more than an inhospitable space. Rather, they hoped to explore the far side of the lake, where, they believed, an almost limitless expanse of ice was available for underground habitation. A daughter of the first line used her influence to secure council approval for the initial exploration. Her name was Mai."

Thea's body reacted to the sound of her mother's name. It was as if a school of tiny fish swam inside of her, everywhere at once. She squeezed her hands into fists and then flexed her fingers, wishing she had thought to bring her ambergris.

"Mai lead three voyages by boat far across the great lake."

Thea braced herself. This would be where her mother died. Mai had drowned during the last charting voyage.

"In several years, the voyagers charted almost the entire perimeter of the lake, but they never came across any place where it was possible to disembark. They met sheer wall all around. The blowers are too heavy to be used from boats afloat on the water, and there was great concern about the possibility of polluting the lake, which is, of course, vital to our survival.

"Mai decided that the new land would have to be reached from the planet's surface, just as the original settlement had been accomplished many years before. Once the new settlement had been established, a connection to Gracehope could be forged. It was a lifetime of work they proposed, but before any of it could begin, they required the council's permission to find a way to the surface."

Thea had to speak.

"Lucian—" She didn't give him time to berate her, but plunged forward, stammering. "That's . . . how can that be? Mai, my mother, died on the last voyage across the lake."

He looked ashen. "It was insensitive of me not to warn you: Your mother did not drown. I am here—I asked to be here—to tell you the truth about how she died."

Thea nodded, her mind reeling.

"There was a good deal of support for the expansion. But there were also many who opposed the notion of surfacing. Grace and the Settlers made a peaceable life possible for us, they said, and to surface, even temporarily, was to jeopardize that life.

"All of this led to a tumultuous political time. The expansion debates, as they were known, were managed well by the Chief of Council, Agis, who was wise enough to move slowly. He called for public debates and a vote, and vowed to act in accord with the judgment of the people.

"Then Agis fell victim to rapid-aging disease. He was dead within months. His niece, Mai's mother, Rowen, presented herself as a successor and was confirmed largely out of blind allegiance to her uncle's memory.

"Rowen was vehemently opposed to the expansion. The public debates soon took on a very different spirit. There was a lot of unpleasantness, always with Mai on one side of the argument and her own mother, Rowen, on the other.

"A full public vote was scheduled according to Agis's original plan. As the date neared, however, fights began to erupt in homes and at workposts. The sides broke down largely along generational lines, and there were several apprentice strikes. There was some fear about what might happen after the vote.

"Then, just before the vote was to take place, Mai walked into the council chamber and, without explanation, withdrew her motion to begin expansion efforts. There would be no vote. There was an outcry from many of her supporters, but without her leadership, the group scattered, unhappy but willing to take up life as it was before.

"What Mai failed to disclose that morning was that she had found—" Lucian faltered—"she had discovered that the Settlers' original migration tunnel had been secretly preserved. The tunnel remained unknown to all but those closest to her."

A group that obviously included Lucian, Thea thought.

"Mai and her Chikchu began making regular trips to the surface."

Gru, Thea realized with a start. Gru had been to the surface with her mother. No wonder the dog had been so unsettled—she was looking for Mai.

"Your mother met someone on the surface, Thea. And befriended him. He was a man of the wider world, a researcher, and the two learned a great deal from each other. Their friendship changed Mai—she came to believe that our people might safely rejoin the wider world.

"But then she fell ill. The nature of her sickness was unknown in Gracehope, and it appeared likely that it was a result of her contact with the surface. She decided to reveal everything to Rowen. But Rowen was more fearful than Mai knew. She used her position as Chief of Council to decree in secret that Mai leave Gracehope until she recovered, claiming that her presence posed a risk to the health of the citizenry.

"Those of us who knew of Rowen's decision were bitterly opposed to it, arguing that there could be no meaningful care for Mai on the cold surface. Rowen was sentencing her own child to death. The conflict nearly erupted into violence"—Lucian colored here, but his voice remained even—"but Mai herself averted that threat and agreed to go."

After a moment he added awkwardly, "She had every hope of returning to Gracehope, and to you, Thea."

Thea kept walking. Each of Lucian's words was a fresh bit of pain, yet she needed him to keep going until the end.

He continued. "Mai was too weak to ascend the tunnel herself. Mai's sister, her closest friend and ally, went with her into the wider world to nurse her, but Mai died only a fortnight later. Rowen announced that she had drowned on a new charting voyage across the lake. Since that time, the tunnel has remained known only to those in whom Mai originally confided. And to Rowen, of course."

Her mother had been exiled to her death. By Rowen. The facts lay inside her, frozen. Thea's mind was a knot. Her only thought was, "Why am I standing here with Lucian, a man who won't even look me in the eye? Why isn't Lana telling me this? Or Sela?" She felt a rush of hatred roll out of her.

She wanted to get away, but the long lake path was

bordered by the water on her left and a sheer wall of ice to the right. There was no way off it. She thought about her mother, sick, being sent away instead of cared for. She thought of the people who had let it happen. Her hands clenched into fists.

There was a sickening spinning in her head, and the trees jumped and waved in front of her. She leaned heavily on the wall next to her, her back flat against it, then turned her cheek to the ice and pressed herself into the cold. She closed her eyes.

She must look ridiculous. She waited for Lucian's scornful remark, and hated him for wanting to be here at all.

But what she felt was warmth. His two hands covering hers. She opened her eyes and found him looking right at her through the hair that fell into his eyes. Tears rolled down his face and dropped to the ground. The sight of him started her own tears.

Neither of them spoke. Lucian kept his hands on hers, and when his tears slowed, he didn't release her to wipe them from his face. After a minute, she stopped crying, too, and could breathe again.

"It is good to allow yourself to feel this pain," Lucian said, still holding her eyes with his. "I wasted a good deal of time trying to deny it. It poisons, after a time. Dexna made me see that, though it took her years."

Thea shook her head and felt a few tears fly off her

face. "But why? Why are you here? Why did you want to be the one to tell me?"

"You mean, what do I have to do with any of this?" Lucian laughed quickly, and then let go of Thea's hands to wipe his cheeks. "You must think me mad."

When Thea was silent, he laughed again. "Fair enough, girl. That's fair enough."

Thea smiled, surprising herself.

Lucian stopped laughing. "I suppose I have left out part of the story. There are two reasons I needed to be here. The first is that I loved your mother, Thea. And she loved me. We . . . we considered ourselves a family, the three of us."

Three: Mai and Lucian, and her. "But you never told me."

Lucian flushed. "After your mother died, I was unwell for a long time. Raving mad, actually."

"And later, when you were better?"

He looked at the ground. "I didn't think you would—"

She cut him off. "What's the second reason? You said there were two."

Lucian seemed to force himself to look at her. "The second reason is that none of it would have happened without me. I told Mai about the tunnel."

"But how did you know of it? Who told you?"

"I guessed. It's right there on the map. But people stopped seeing it."

"So it was you who left me the map."

"No." Lucian shook his head. "I was opposed, in truth. It was Dexna who left it. That map has been passed down among the daughters of the first line since the time of Settlement. But somewhere along the way they forgot why."

"Grace's Hope," Thea said.

Lucian nodded. "It seems that Grace had many hopes. One was that this world could exist. And another was that our people would one day abandon it. The tunnel was preserved in secret—there are no records of it. Grace's granddaughter Sarah drew a map that was deliberately vague, and then its meaning was lost."

"Until you discovered it," Thea said.

Lucian nodded. "When your mother turned sixteen she told me that Dexna had given her a copy of one of the settlement maps. It was to be passed to a daughter of each generation, but she didn't know why. And I wondered, what is the use of a tradition without meaning? So I looked for a meaning, and Mai died as a result."

"You didn't know what would happen," Thea said. She wasn't sure if she was reassuring Lucian or trying to convince herself.

Lucian scraped one foot on the ground. "No, I couldn't know. But I have found that to be little comfort. You look cold. Shall we walk again?"

Thea walked, her mind struggling with everything Lucian had told her, until one thought worked itself free of the others.

"I have a question." A hundred questions.

"Yes?"

"You said my mother's sister went with her into exile, to nurse her."

He said the word more slowly this time. "Yes."

"But Lana is my mother's sister. She told me just yesterday that she has never been to the wider world. She wouldn't lie to me." But she had, Thea realized. Lana had lied about everything.

Lucian met Thea's eyes. "Lana is one of your mother's sisters. There was another."

"Another sister? How? Even Rowen wouldn't have been permitted a third birth."

"Mai had a birth-sister," Lucian said gently. "They were born together. One birth."

Thea's hand went slowly to the locket at her throat. She opened it and looked at the tiny rendering of the three girls that she had studied so many times before: Lana, Mai, and the other girl, who Thea had always believed was Sela. How had she failed to see it?

"What's her name?" Thea asked, her finger tracing the form of the girl.

"Her name was Aurora."

Was. "Why does no one speak of her? Did she . . . did she die, too?"

"We don't know. She never returned to us. Rowen

234

announced that she took her own life after your mother died."

"She never returned?" Thea asked. "Then how do you know that . . . are you sure my mother is dead? Who came to tell you of it?"

"There was a letter from Aurora, sent down the tunnel with their Chikchu. Gru, of course, and Aurora's companion, Norma."

Norma. Norma, who cried at night, who wouldn't let Dolan out of her sight. For some reason, this was the revelation that started Thea's tears again. She felt Lucian take her hand.

They continued walking in silence until they reached the end of the path, the place where the narrow shore melted into the wall and disappeared altogether. Thea hugged the last tree and looked across the lake.

"Your mother was fascinated by this spot," Lucian said after a while. "She called it the end of the world."

TWENTY-SIX

PETER

There was a roaring now, somewhere close and coming closer. Peter's mind roused itself a little, but the pain and tumult were too much to bear. He fell back into peaceful oblivion before he could realize that he had been lifted from the snow and was being carried.

TWENTY-SEVEN

THEA

Thea wanted desperately to be alone for a time, to sit under the trees at the lake, look at the still water, and think about everything Lucian had told her. But she was due at the breeding grounds, and she didn't want to disappoint Dolan again.

Her mother's life, her mother's death: She had been lied to by the people closest to her, people who now expected her to understand. Worse, she had been taught to respect the woman who had exiled her mother to her death. She had been made to bow politely to her, to serve her the tea that Lana saved so carefully. Her loathing for Rowen churned inside her.

She skated furiously down the Mainway and arrived at the breeding grounds, her mind ablaze with angry questions.

Dolan wasn't in the main house, where she threw her skates down and grabbed up some clean straw for the pups. She could feel how keenly she had missed them.

The pups were asleep, the runt in his usual spot under Cassie's chin. Their faces were so peaceful, their confidence in their mother and their world so pure, that Thea was overwhelmed with sadness. She threw her arms around Cassie and buried her face in the big Chikchu's fur.

Cassie nuzzled her, trying to settle Thea the way she did her pups. Before long Thea's breathing slowed, her head rising and falling with Cassie's broad back.

"Feeling better today?"

Thea lifted her head with a jerk. "I'm sorry I lied to you, Dolan," she blurted. "From now on I'm going to speak only the truth! And I don't care how inconvenient the truth is."

Dolan sat next to her in the sand. "I've always had a fondness for the truth myself," he said gently. He put one hand on her shoulder and squeezed it quickly.

They sat saying nothing more until the children arrived

at the main house to meet Cassie's litter. Dolan stood and crossed the sands to admit them.

Thea looked carefully at each pup as the group struggled to wake. Io was the steadiest, her eyes clear and her balance much improved. The others were coming along, tripping over one another a bit more, but ready to meet their companions. At first Thea thought that the runt was slow to rouse, but then she realized with a small shock that the pup had not yet opened his eyes. He stood steadily enough, but leaned his body against his mother's flank.

Thea lifted him gently, gathered his legs into her cupped hands to make him feel secure, and then checked him over. He looked perfect, but his eyes stayed closed.

Dolan stopped a short distance from where Thea sat with the tiny pup still in her hands, and told the children to wait. She counted quickly: there were only seven of them. He crossed to her.

"I'll take the runt for now," he said in a low voice. "If his eyes open within a sevennight, you can make the introduction then."

"And if they don't?" She passed the pup into his hands.

But Dolan just shook his head.

After the assembly, she skated home slowly, letting her muscles warm and stretch. It hadn't occurred to Thea that her aunt would be back from the gardens, as it was still well before suppertime. But when she walked into the greatroom, Lana looked up from her worktable.

"I'll warm some water for us," she said quickly.

Thea felt cold. She just wanted to be alone. "I'd rather sleep first, I think."

"You've had plenty of sleep," Lana said. "What we need is some sweet ricewater."

"I've had enough of your ricewater, thanks."

But Lana was already filling a small pot from the pump. "It won't be that sort, I promise. You and I need to talk." She gestured Thea to a seat at the long table.

Thea didn't move. "What do you want me to say?"

"I can see that you are angry."

"Shouldn't I be?"

Lana looked startled. "Yes. You should."

Thea was disgusted with everyone except Mattias and Dolan. And she was especially angry with Lana. "Really, I'd much rather . . ."

"Thea. Please have one cup with me. Then I'll let you go."

Thea realized with a shock that her aunt looked about to cry. She couldn't remember Lana ever crying. She sat down.

"I know you are upset with me, and I know why." Lana sat next to Thea. "But say it anyway, so we'll have a place to start."

Thea looked away. "I *knew* her, in a way," she said. "In my way. And now she's a stranger again. You've kept her a stranger to me all along."

"Everything I've ever told you about your mother is true to her spirit."

"But you've hardly told me anything! Did you know that I used to talk to her, by the lake? Because I thought she was *there,* somewhere, but I was only talking to water, and fish, and ice. And you let me. You *let* me."

That started Thea's tears again. Lana took both of her hands.

"I'm sorrier than you'll ever know."

"But why? Why did you allow all of those lies, the ones about the tunnel, and about my mother? And Aurora? How could you let one of your sisters be forgotten?"

Lana was silent for a while. And then she said, "There's something I want to show you." Lana crossed to her worktable, opened a wide drawer and, reaching all the way to the back of it, withdrew a scrap of paper.

She held it out. Thea took it and read:

Here under and aboute the pole is beste habitation for man, and that they ever have continuall daye, and know not what night or darkness meaneth.

Thea looked up, wiping her eyes. "What does this have to do with anything?"

Lana sat down at the long table again. "It's a line from

a letter, written by an early explorer of the cold world. He was here long before our people came to this part of the world. His ship arrived during the summer, when the sun shines both day and night. Not yet understanding the sun's cycle, he believed that he had discovered a land of perpetual daylight. A world without darkness."

Thea looked blankly at her aunt.

Lana continued. "I'm sure Lucian has the letter somewhere among his heaps—I saw it once, years ago, during my primary studies. I copied this line down and have kept it all this time. Something about it touched me, this man's childlike belief that he had found something magical—a land of continual day."

"But there's no such thing," said Thea.

Lana smiled. "You're right. There isn't. What I think, Thea, is that I was determined to create a kind of continual day, for you. A false light." She shook her head slowly. "All of us tried to do that, I think, in our own ways. Except Dexna, of course."

"What do you mean?" asked Thea.

"Dexna's silence is a protest, one that's lasted almost fourteen years now. It's her way of remembering your mother. And her way of reminding others."

Lana reached out and wrapped one hand around Thea's forearm. "What happened was almost too much for me to bear. I told myself that you would be happier without the knowledge of such a bitter past, such . . .

darkness. But I see now that I was doing it for myself. It made my life so much easier, you see, to act as if none of it had happened. It made life possible for me."

Thea nodded, her throat closed up painfully. Seeing tears in Lana's eyes, she could feel her own starting again.

"I told myself I was protecting you," Lana said, "but I was teaching you lies, and doing it to comfort myself. I can't tell you how sorry I am, because you bear such a burden, you had to grow up without a mother, and you deserved to be raised in truth."

Thea began crying hard then, but found her voice somehow. "I didn't, Lana. I didn't grow up without a mother!"

Then they were both weeping, Lana with her arms wrapped around Thea, who was still clutching the worn scrap in her hand. Neither of them moved when the pot began to boil on the fire.

TWENTY-EIGHT

THEA

Lana had persuaded Thea to rest awhile before supper. She had stripped to her tunic and leggings and was rearranging her bedclothes when she heard the dock-door bell. It must be Dolan arriving with Peg! Thea ran into the greatroom just as Lana swung the door open.

Then Thea heard something she had never heard before: Lana screamed.

Her aunt fell to her knees, and Thea saw a woman in the doorway.

TWENTY-NINE

PETER

Though his eyes were closed, Peter was slowly becoming aware of a light. He didn't move at first, but tried to feel around his brain to see if he could figure out where he was or what had happened. He remembered seeing the ice wall in the distance, and lying down in the snow.

"He's waking," a voice said.

Peter knew the voice. From where? Where was he? He wanted to open his eyes, but was strangely unsure how to go about it. Why couldn't he think?

His brain seized on a sound: a low thrumming.

The sound of Thea's place.

The next thing that came to him: someone was holding his hand.

He started to turn his head, to open his eyes.

"Not yet." The voice was sharp. "Let me adjust the light."

It was the woman who had met him and Thea at the bottom of the tunnel. The woman with the bracelets.

"All right, try to open your eyes. Slowly."

Peter's eyelids felt heavy, as if a hand were pressing down on them. He raised them carefully. He could make out very little—two lights burning fuzzily near the foot of the bed, a couple of figures standing behind them.

Someone was squeezing his hand. He turned his head. Thea?

But the person next to him, her face streaming with tears, was his mother.

"You had me scared, Peter," she said. "As scared as I've ever been."

There was a snort from behind her. "*You* were scared? Imagine what you put the boy through, Aurora—no warning whatsoever, no guidance . . ."

Peter found his voice. "How did we get here? How do you know about this place?"

His mother raised Peter's hand to her face and kissed it.

"I was born here, Peter. Gracehope was my home."

THIRTY

THEA

S ome things never change, Thea thought, and for once she was grateful.

Life was new in ways beyond imagining: Aurora had reappeared as if summoned by Thea's knowledge of her. Peter was Aurora's son, Thea's own cousin.

Dexna had hidden them both at the archive and warned that no one could know they were here. Dexna said "no one" in a way that was frightening.

But the Chikchu still whelped in the middle of the night. Dolan had summoned Thea by messenger just a few hours after Aurora appeared at Lana's dock door. The next morning, she was still at the breeding grounds. She rubbed her stiff neck. She hadn't even seen Mattias yet.

Thea had been ready to go home when Dexna appeared at the breeding grounds with Peg, Ham, and Sasha, and announced that Peter's dog would have to be hidden somewhere. Then she took Dolan away with her, leaving Thea to clean up the mess from the whelping. When she was done with that, Thea realized that Cassie needed clean bedding as well. And then the dogs in the main house were hungry again. Finally, she had dozed off in a clean pile of straw. She sighed. No wonder Dolan slept here so often. He probably didn't have the energy to get himself home.

Thea carefully lifted each pup from Cassie's whelping box, checking it over before replacing it next to its mother. They had become a playful bunch, rolling around and nipping at one another until Cassie had had enough and gotten up to take a walk. She examined the runt last, cupping the wriggling thing in one hand while he groped blindly for his mother. She told herself it wasn't time to worry yet. A sevennight, Dolan had said. They had six more days to hope.

She sat with Peg for a few minutes and looked at Ham and Sasha, who were stretched out next to each other at her feet. Peg put her face in Thea's lap and closed her eyes. The thought of joining her in a nap was tempting.

But she had to see Mattias. And Peter, and Aurora. She forced herself up and started home.

Thea opened her door to find Lana's greatroom table covered with dishes of food. Sela and Lana were at the counter mixing a pitcher of tea. Thea stooped to flip up her skate blades. If Rowen is here, she told herself, I'm leaving.

Mattias! He sat on a bench near Lana's worktable with his back against the wall, looking tired and holding a red drink. Thea ran to embrace him, nearly knocking the cup from his hand.

"Careful!" Lana called. "There are more rushberries in that drink than I had rations for." She held an identical cup out to Thea.

Thea took the drink carefully. It was delicious, tart and sweet. Mattias was grinning up at her now, and patting the bench beside him. "This is my second one," he said quietly. "I should nearly freeze to death more often."

"Don't," Thea said, leaning hard against him.

A moment later, the dock door opened and Dexna stepped through it. "It is time for us to make some decisions," she announced.

Thea looked at Mattias next to her. "No 'good morning'?" she whispered.

"She takes getting used to."

Sela waved Thea and Mattias to the long table. "Losh,

Mother," Sela said, piling riceflats onto their plates, "so much has happened. What sort of decisions did you have in mind?"

Dexna gave Sela a steely look. "Different decisions. With hope, better ones."

Lana walked around the table filling glasses from a water pitcher. She gave Thea's shoulder a squeeze as she passed.

"My mother's first mistake was trusting Rowen," Thea said. She waited for someone to tell her she shouldn't be talking this way. But everyone was silent. "And her second mistake was keeping the tunnel a secret. People have a right to know."

"Many won't like the idea of it," Sela said. "A way out is the same as a way in. It will make some feel vulnerable."

Mattias nodded. "Exposed."

Dexna leaned forward. "That's why we must tell everyone about the passage *before* Rowen can make them fear it. They must see it as a sign of hope, of a future."

Thea spoke before thinking: "The legend pup!"

Sela squealed and grabbed Thea's arm. "The legend pup. Brilliant. I have chills! The legend pup along with the discovery of the passage is as good as Grace herself explaining what she meant all along."

Thea wished she hadn't spoken so quickly. She heard Dolan's warning voice in her head: *A sevennight.* What would people make of a blind legend pup? She wasn't sure she liked the omen herself.

"Should we call a citizens' meeting?" Thea asked.

"Absolutely not!" Dexna shook her head. "Rowen will immediately guess why, destroy the passage, and make herself a hero for doing so. She must suspect nothing."

"There's a council meeting in a fortnight," Thea said.

"Too long to wait," said Dexna.

Lana spoke for the first time. "Are you all forgetting that tomorrow is Launch?"

No one said anything.

"Everyone will be there," Lana said. "Is there any other choice?"

"We are decided," said Dexna.

Sela cleared the table. "Dolan knows about all of this, doesn't he?" Thea asked her. "He doesn't talk about it."

Sela was on her way to the basin with a stack of dirty plates. "He knows, sweet. But Dolan just wants to be where the dogs are. You know that."

"And on the subject of dogs," Dexna said to Thea in a low voice when they were alone at the table. "Let's see what you can do about that runt of yours who won't open his eyes. And if there is nothing you can do, it would be better not to speak of him again."

THIRTY-ONE

Peter woke. His right hand flexed, but his mother wasn't there holding on to him as she had been for the last . . . how many hours? He had no idea.

His headache was nothing more than a quiet droning now, a fire engine that had shrieked its way down Sixth Avenue, almost gone. His head felt light on the pillow.

But it wasn't a pillow, exactly. He probed the thing under his head with one hand. It was more like a cloth bag full of plants. And it smelled like plants—something like the tea his mother had to have every morning before she could put three words together. Where was she, anyway?

Warm, he kicked off the thick blanket. He was wearing clothes that didn't belong to him. They were pale blue, thin and clingy, something like long johns. Pajamas? He ran one hand through his hair.

The room was dim, but he could make out stacks of books and papers on the floor. The chair next to his bed held the sketch his mom had shown him the night before: her twin sister, the one who died before he was born. Thea's mother.

Orange light spilled in through an open archway, but Peter heard nothing from the other side of it. Was he alone? He got up, frowning at his thick socks—also baby blue—and picked his way through the piles toward the light. He looked into a room full of books, benches, and tables.

Dexna glanced up from a book. "Better now?"

"Yes, I think so." There was a long counter against one wall. A covered pot sat on the counter next to a basket of bread. He was hungry. Very.

"About time," Dexna said, following his gaze. "I was beginning to wonder whether your mother would spend another evening spooning broth into you."

Peter blushed.

"Help yourself. I've set out a bowl for you."

On the counter he found a bowl and a spoon, along with a cloth napkin.

The bowl was heavier than he expected. He held it up

to the lamp that hung from a peg on the wall. A light-globe, Thea had called it in the tunnel. He turned the bowl with one hand. It was translucent.

"It's ice," Dexna said from her bench.

"Ice?" Peter lowered the bowl to the counter. "But it's—"

"Not cold?" She looked at him. "That's because it's sealed ice—ice made permanent, almost like rock."

It did feel like ice, Peter thought, if ice could be imagined dry and warm. He looked at the spoon on the counter. Same stuff. "I'd like to see that sometime," he said, peering into the pot. Some sort of soup. It smelled fishy.

Dexna grunted. "It's not very interesting—much like watching someone paint a fence. Sealant is an acid; it burns. And it's smelly."

"Who discovered it?" Peter served himself from the pot.

"Our founder, Grace, did. She was a particular sort of genius."

"Did she invent the lights, too?" Peter gestured to the lightglobe.

Dexna nodded. "For the light you can thank Grace and the fireflies that taught her."

So that's why the light was green, Peter thought.

"Do you guys have telephones?" He sat down and began to eat.

Dexna smiled. "No. What do telephones do?"

"They're machines that let people talk to each other, from far away."

Dexna looked interested. "Is that so? Well, here we have messengers." She smiled. "Do you skate?"

Peter nodded. "My mom and I go all the time, in the winter." He stopped. His mother was an amazing skater. A lot of things like that were beginning to fall into place.

He took a piece of bread from the counter. It was nearly a rock.

"Yesterday's bake," Dexna said unapologetically. "Try dipping it into your soup."

He pushed the bread into his soup. Much better. He began to eat. It was pretty good, like French onion soup, with fish.

"Do you think I could borrow some skates?"

Dexna looked surprised. "I'll find a pair of skates for you. But you won't be able to use them just yet."

"Why not? I feel fine." His headache had disappeared.

"That is not the issue. It cannot be known that you are here. Not yet."

So he still wasn't supposed to be here. "Do you know where my mother is?"

"Yes," Dexna said. "And I promised that I would take you to her."

"Can we go now?"

Dexna tossed him a fur. She took one from a peg for herself, and Peter watched closely as her fingers flew over a series of ties. He did his best to copy her, but had trouble with the strings on his coat. It was different from the one Thea had lent him. He looked more closely. It almost seemed like—

"Yes, the fur is Chikchu," Dexna said gruffly. "We haven't any choice. But each of them lives a long life, and dies naturally. And we wear the fur with respect."

Peter tried not to think about it. There were also worn brown boots to put on. Now that he was dressed, the heat of the little room was stifling.

Dexna pointed to the bench by the door. "Sit while I get the dogs harnessed."

"I can help—"

"No. Stay out of sight. I'll be back soon."

Peter sat on the bench, sweating, until Dexna came back and waved him through another room—more benches and tables, still hot—to a beat-up wooden door set neatly into a blue wall of ice. The door looked ancient— he ran one hand over it.

"Wood," Dexna said, looking proud. "From the whaling ship that brought our people here from England."

"Did they land here by accident?" Peter asked. His father had told him that sometimes people were stranded in Greenland when their boats broke up on the ice.

"Of course not. They planned to come here. They were running for their lives!" Dexna shook her head. "I apologize. It isn't your fault you know nothing of it."

Whose fault was it, Peter wondered as she swung the door open. He looked to see how it worked—hinges. No mystery there.

Just as he was about to get his first gulp of cool air, Dexna reached out and pulled his hood over his head. She looked up and down the icy path and pointed to the floor of the sleigh in front of them. It was wood, too, even more worn than the door.

"Lie down, please."

Peter was facedown in the sleigh with Dexna's feet on either side of his shoulders, a woven blanket draped over him. Through the slats of the sleigh he watched the grainy ice speeding by beneath them. He tried to push himself up on his elbows but felt Dexna's foot between his shoulder blades.

"My apologies," she said quietly. "We are nearly to the Mainway crossing."

He put his head down again and felt Dexna rearrange the blanket. A few moments later they stopped, and then lurched forward again.

When they had ridden for a while, Dexna began to speak.

"Our people were English," she said quietly, "always

close to the land and its ways. They knew how to grow things, and how to raise healthy animals. And some of them had . . . gifts. For this they were hunted by ignorant folk who accused them of witchcraft. They were nearly extinguished. Those who survived came here, where they might live in peace."

"*Are* you— I mean we . . ." He couldn't quite bring himself to finish the question. It was ridiculous enough trying to talk from underneath a blanket.

"Witches?" Dexna laughed as if she liked the sound of that. "Of course not. But our gifts were noticed—the ability to hear beyond the normal range is most common, and there are other things, uncommon intelligence, like Grace's. Or exceptional sight, like yours."

So she knew. "How did you—"

"I knew the minute I saw the blacks of your eyes, shrunk to almost nothing. That, and the fact that you fainted. Fainting is said to be typical."

The sleigh stopped, and Dexna lifted the blanket from Peter's head. It was a relief. He raised his head cautiously and saw that they had stopped at a dead end—the path ended in two wide wooden doors.

"The records say that eye adepts had the hardest time during emergence," Dexna said, "and males especially so. But I think the worst of yours is over now."

"Eye adepts." He tried the name on.

"Yes, that's what they were called."

"*Were* called?"

Dexna hesitated. "There hasn't been an eye adept among us for a very long time."

"But . . . why not?" Great. He was a freak among freaks.

She shrugged. "We can't be sure. I'd like to work with you, to help you learn how to use your sight. I've started to do some research. I found a few old journal entries. It's better than nothing."

Peter was washed with relief. Yes! Someone was going to help him. He'd been feeling his way through this thing for too long.

"That would be great. And who knows, there may be other eye adepts somewhere, in the . . ." He pointed up, but stopped himself before he said the words "real world."

"We call it the wider world," Dexna said. "And there is no one else. Gracehope was settled a long time ago, Peter. Your mother and Mai were the first people to leave."

"Is my mom here?"

Dexna nodded as one of the big doors opened and a heavyset man with short dark hair appeared. Peter had a vague memory of the same man coming to see him the night before, standing in the corner for a moment before rushing out again.

"This is my son, Dolan," Dexna said, "and these are

the Chikchu breeding grounds. Your mother used to spend most of her time here." She gave another *tsk* and the dogs lurched eagerly forward. This is a place dogs like to be, Peter thought as the sleigh drew inside. Dolan closed the door and slid a lock into place.

"Come on then," Dolan said. He leaned forward, smiling. "Out with you."

Peter scrambled up awkwardly.

"You're looking much improved today." Dolan peered at Peter.

"Much better today," Peter said. "It was . . . a headache, really. A bad one, but it's gone now."

Dolan nodded. "Eye adept. I heard."

Peter looked around. They were in a large shed. A bunch of dogs were sitting or lying down inside little stalls, like something for horses. A few of them had splinted legs.

"Your mother is out there among the pups." Dolan pointed through a set of large doors in the far wall. Beyond them, Peter could see a dimly lit area, lightglobes turned down to a deep color that reminded him of the last of a fire. Little clusters of dogs were here and there. His mother sat near a big dog.

He practically ran.

"Peter!" His mother smiled widely and held out an arm to bring him in toward her. He sat down and let her hug him. It was a minute before he noticed the tiny puppy in her lap. Dark gray or black—it was hard to tell in the half-light—with white paws.

"He's a runt," she said. "Hers." She pointed at a pretty dog across the sand who was nursing several other pups. "I can't take him too far. She's got her eye on me."

Peter rearranged himself so that he didn't obscure the dog's view of her baby.

"And this is Norma." His mother rubbed the big black dog stretched out on her other side. "She's an old friend." Next to Norma was his mother's red notebook.

She looked at him closely. "How's the head?"

"Better. Much better. Sorry I kept falling asleep last night."

"Don't be silly." She rubbed the puppy behind the ears. "You needed to sleep."

"I was going to tell you," Peter started.

She nodded. "About your sight? Or about stumbling across this place?"

"Both. I think."

"I suppose there's a lot we could have told each other."

"How did you know that I was out there? In the snow?"

"I heard Sasha calling—she sort of brought me back."

"She did? So do you— Does that mean that you can hear dogs, like Thea?"

"Yes. I've been an ear adept since I was about your age."

"Did you get the headaches, too?"

"I had them. Headaches are usually the first sign, for ear adepts. Apparently they are much worse for eye adepts. I had no idea what you were going through, Peter. I wish you had told me."

"And the other kind of headache . . . the kind you had yesterday, back in camp. Those aren't really headaches at all, are they?"

His mother looked down. "No. Sometimes I need to . . . withdraw, I suppose. I have all of this sorrow inside me. At times I can hardly move." She met his eyes. "I guess it felt easier to give it a name. I'm sorry."

Peter felt as if someone had just told him he could finally put down the two-ton boulder he'd been lugging around. He smiled at his mom and scooped up a handful of rough sand, letting it run through his fingers. "So what's it like, being an ear adept?"

"All it means is that I can hear a wider range of sounds than most people, including the ones that the Chikchu use to communicate. I studied their signals. It's sort of like memorizing Morse code. What's it like being an eye adept?"

"Pretty cool. I can sort of zoom in on things. I'm not very good at it yet, though." He looked around. "Dexna says you used to spend a lot of your time here."

"I was Dolan's first apprentice. Second-in-charge, that means."

She had always told Peter she raised dogs as a child in

England. The half-truth of that rankled inside him. What else didn't he know yet?

"Where are your parents?" he asked suddenly. She'd always said they died before Peter was born.

"My mother, Rowen, is here. I don't know who my father is."

"Can I meet your mom?"

She shook her head slowly. "She's a very difficult person. Not like your friends' grandparents at all. Now is not the time for you to meet. I'm so sorry." Another apology. He felt a gush of anger. She seemed to think that saying "I'm sorry" could make up for all of her lies. He pushed the feeling away and looked at the puppy in her lap.

"Got any more of those lying around here?"

She broke into a grin. "How thoughtless of me."

She showed him how to hold the tiny puppy so that it would feel safe. He hadn't realized it couldn't see yet. Peter cradled it in the crook of his arm, rubbing its head with one finger. It felt good to have something to hold on to.

"So this is what your book is about, right? Mitochondrial DNA?"

His mother smiled. "Yes. One woman—her name was Grace, she was your great-grandmother's great-grandmother, or something like that—figured out a lot of this science, and the world is starting to catch up with her a little. I was trying to put some of the pieces together for myself."

"And the bracelets—the ones that Dexna wears . . ."

"They look a lot like mitochondrial DNA. Grace was fond of leaving clues."

"But how? She couldn't have known what it looks like! Way back then?"

"It *is* hard to believe. But I can't think of any other explanation for it. I think she must have known things that science hasn't even discovered yet." His mother sighed. "I wish she'd written more of it down."

"Weird. So can you understand dogs at home? I mean, in New York?"

"Peter. New York *is* my home now. My only home. And no, I've never heard anything like a signal from a dog that wasn't a Chikchu. That was the amazing thing. When you blacked out, Sasha used a Chikchu call. It's an S.O.S. signal down here. I thought it was a Chikchu calling. Instead, I found Sasha, wrapped around you."

Peter shook his head. "She must have learned it from Thea's dogs, when they were calling for help for Mattias."

His mother nodded. "Dolan thinks so, too."

"Sasha's pretty amazing."

"Yes." She was quiet for a minute. Then she said, "After everything that's happened, maybe we could have Daddy talk to someone about keeping Sasha."

"Really? You mean bring her home?"

"If we can get permission to keep her in the apartment."

Peter imagined Sasha stretched out on his loft, lying in the square of light that came through the skylight in the afternoons. It seemed like the most natural thing in the world. And then his mind switched gears.

"Did you tell Dad you were leaving? He must be so worried."

His mom nodded. "I didn't get to speak with him. But we had a plan worked out—you know Daddy, he's nothing if not a planner. There was a signal: a red flashlight, upside down on the table. I left it there when I heard Sasha's call."

"The red flashlight," Peter said, remembering the box of black flashlights back in New York, with the one red one sitting right in the middle.

She smiled. "It meant that I had found Gracehope."

"You didn't know where it was," Peter said slowly. Now it all made sense.

"No, I couldn't find it. It's moved, along with a huge piece of the ice sheet, it seems."

"Moved where?"

"West. Toward the sea."

"You mean the whole thing is sliding into the ocean?" He found himself whispering.

"Well, yes, but slowly. Just not as slowly as we thought."

"Let me guess: global warming."

She smiled. "Now you know the whole story."

Hardly, he thought. "How did you get me down here?"

"Sasha led me. I was trying to bring you back to camp, but she kept running in the other direction."

"What's Daddy supposed to tell Jonas? That we went for a really long walk?"

"I don't know. Maybe that we decided to go to Qaanaaq, or out exploring."

"Won't Jonas think that's strange? Yesterday you couldn't even get out of bed."

She shrugged. "Probably. We'll be back in a few hours, anyway. We'll figure out something to tell him."

"A few hours? What are you talking about? We just got here!"

She frowned. "We can't stay. Dexna is planning to tell everyone about the tunnel tomorrow morning."

"So?"

"They may choose to destroy it, Peter. We have to leave while we can."

"Destroy it? But didn't you tell them that the ice is moving?" That was why they had come to Greenland, he realized. He sat up with a start. To tell these people what was happening.

"Yes, I told Dexna what we know. But people here fear the wider world. I don't know what they'll do."

Peter shook his head. "But Dexna wants to teach me

about being an eye adept! And I haven't even seen Gracehope! This is about me, too! You're not being fair!"

"I'm protecting you! That's my job!" His mother put her face into her hands, and Peter realized that this must have been one of the things she was afraid of, that he would want to stay. He thought of the note he found under their couch in New York. *What's the worst that can happen?*

"Mom?"

She lifted her head.

"Just one more day," he said. "We'll be okay here for one day. And Dad will understand."

She looked at him for a long time, and then she nodded.

THIRTY-TWO

PETER

An hour later, Peter was watching a dog sing. Or that was what Thea told him the dog was doing. He didn't hear a sound.

"Not very good, is she?" Thea had her hands over her ears.

Peter's mother was wincing. "Well, that settles that," she said to Peter. "An ear adept you aren't. You'll have to settle for being the first seer in two centuries."

Thea showed the dog a quick hand sign and it trotted happily away.

"What was that?" Peter asked, trying to imitate her splayed fingers.

"This?" Thea laughed, forming the sign again. "It means 'food.' I'll teach you. You'll have any Chikchu in Gracehope doing your bidding by tomorrow afternoon."

Except that he wouldn't be here tomorrow afternoon.

"Will you be all right here until Dexna comes?" his mother asked him. "Thea has promised to take me to the gardens."

It was some consolation that he wasn't the only one who had to ride around facedown in the bottom of a sled. He nodded. "I'll be fine, Mom."

When his mother started for the main house, Peter went to find the runt. The tiny Chikchu was curled up in his usual spot under Cassie's chin while the other puppies tumbled around on the sand or nursed.

"Lazy," Peter said, looking down at him.

Cassie lifted her head and gave a quiet sniff, reminding Peter to offer her his hand. "I didn't mean you."

The runt stirred and woke, then went through a series of stretches and yawns so elaborate that Peter laughed out loud.

"Come on, little white feet," he said, scooping up the pup with one hand, "you can't sleep your life away in a box." Peter held the dog close to his face, and the puppy kneaded his cheek with his two front paws. His mother said that it was good for the puppies to get used to people. When the runt opened his eyes—any day now, Thea said firmly—he would have a companion to visit him like his brothers and sisters did, but for now Peter was more than happy to have the job. He set the dog down in the sand and tickled his belly.

"I can't hear you," he told the pup, who had rolled onto his back. "But I hope you're laughing."

Before long, Dexna made her way across the sands, a book under one arm. He put the runt back with his mother and stood up.

She nodded at him. Peter knew that she spoke to very few people, and was grateful that she talked to him at all. He wasn't sure he would be able to bear this woman in complete silence.

Dexna took off her bright green wrap, gathered her skirts, and sat next to him. She must have come by sled—sleigh, he corrected himself. No one skated in skirts, according to Thea.

"Let's begin." Dexna smiled at him. She had a really warm smile. The smile went with her eyes, and her clothes.

Peter nodded and closed his eyes for a moment. Then he opened them slowly.

"Look at the main house," she said. "Do you see the harness pegs along the beam?"

He turned his gaze to the main house, where the doors

leading onto the sands stood wide open. The outer doors, the ones leading to the Mainway and the rest of Gracehope, were barred. They always were, when Peter was here.

A smooth wooden beam ran across the ceiling of the main house. Another piece of the whaling ship, he supposed. All sorts of things hung from it on hooks and pegs—tools, lightglobes, and netted bags.

"I see them."

"One of the pegs is different from the others," Dexna said.

That was his task, then. Peter held his gaze steady, stilling his eyes and trying not to blink. Soon the fluttering began, just at the very edges of his vision. The movement was almost lazy at first. He waited.

The shimmering moved like a contracting lens, reaching in toward the place he held his gaze. The wooden beam. The pegs on the beam. Everything around them was weaving now, as if he were looking through some terrific heat. An invisible inferno.

Then Dolan walked into the scene, carrying a stack of woven blankets. Peter's gaze broke toward him for a second. The fluttering was gone. He blinked and sighed. At least there was no headache yet. "Dolan came in."

Dexna nodded. "I asked him to walk about a little. You must learn how to ignore distractions."

Peter started again. This time it went quickly. In less

271

than half a minute, he was staring at the grain of the wooden beam. Too close.

Pulling back was difficult. It caused an ache across the tops of his eyes, as if he were trying to roll them back into his head. He stretched his sight away from the wood grain until he had a view of a peg, then two pegs, then three. He could see the stretched material of the hanging harnesses, and stains left by the animals' sweat.

He looked carefully at the pegs, all of them sealed ice—Peter could recognize the grayish sheen of the stuff now. He moved down the row, panning like a movie camera, until the last peg came into his circle of vision. Light bounced off of it so painfully he couldn't believe he hadn't seen it straight away. Someone must polish it regularly.

"The last peg is metal," he said with satisfaction. "Brass?"

"Yes," Dexna said.

Peter smiled. "What's next?"

Dexna sighed. "I don't know. Much of this knowledge was taken for granted once. Let's try another one."

By the time Dexna left an hour later, Peter was tired. He felt a slight pressure behind his eyes, but had managed not to get a headache, which meant he was doing everything right, Dexna said.

She had offered him a ride back to the archive, but

Peter wasn't ready for the closeness and the warmth of that place. Instead, he helped Dolan load three sleighs with sacks and sacks of food for the Chikchu. Errand boys would deliver them to the companion shelters later. Peter was pretty sure that delivering dog food wasn't a job many people would jump for, but he thought of those boys jealously. So far, the breeding grounds and the archive were the only two places he had been allowed. Thea had offered to take him skating on the backways in the dead of night, but Dexna shook her head.

When the sleighs were loaded and ready to go, Peter sat with Sasha in the main house. He had begun to tell her about New York: He described his loft, where they would both sleep, and the dog run where he would take her every afternoon, and he told her the names of the dogs he knew around the neighborhood, the ones his mother had made friends with over the years. There was a German shepherd named Maggie that he thought Sasha would especially like. Peter sat cross-legged and talked, and Sasha leaned hard against him until he took the hint and rubbed her chest.

A bell sounded, and Dolan asked him, apologetically, to step out onto the sands so that he could open the front doors. The errand boys had arrived to pick up their deliveries.

The runt's mom was off somewhere, and a few of the

puppies were play-fighting in the whelping box. Peter found the runt alone, a few feet from the box. He watched the tiny dog lurch around on the sand. The poor thing couldn't seem to find his way back home.

"You're going the wrong way, Feet," Peter said. "I thought you guys could hear each other." Peter scooped up the puppy and held him up to his face for a moment before sitting down with him on the sand.

The bigger pups were rolling around in the whelping box. Peter began to narrate the action for Feet. It was something Miles did when he was practicing to be a sportscaster.

"Black's on top! He's rolled Stripes onto his back—no, Stripes is up, he's backing Black into a corner. White is in there now—she's jumped on both of them, she's all over the place, oops, she's rolled out of the box. Okay, White's back, she's in again. No, wait, she's walking away. White's curled up in the corner! C'mon, White, get back in the game!"

Feet sat up in Peter's lap, his face tilted toward the sound of Peter's voice until Cassie came back and put an end to her puppies' wrestling.

Exhaustion settled slowly over Peter, and after a while he stretched out next to the whelping box and looked at the tiny dog next to him. "You have to work on opening your eyes, okay, Feet? Thea says it's important. We'll both work on our eyes. You and me. Now go on back to your mom." He rested his head on one arm and watched the puppy.

"Go on. I don't want you wandering off again. Your mom is waiting." But when Peter's eyes closed a few minutes later, the puppy was still beside him.

THIRTY-THREE

THEA

Thea had been listening to Aurora and Lana talk for nearly two hours. Her aunts. These are my two aunts, she said to herself. My mother's sisters. She still found it strange to look at Aurora: It was like seeing Lana and Mai mixed up together.

The greenhouse where Lana bred her plants was wet and warm, and the three of them had stripped off their furs and twisted their hair up on top of their heads, pinning it there with the sticks Lana used to stake her smallest plants. While they talked, Lana walked among her flowers, stopping to pinch a few leaves off one or to spray water mist on another with a tiny pump she kept in the pocket of her apron. Thea stayed out of the way, sitting on a low stool and kneading her knot of ambergris. She had discovered long ago that she could often learn more by holding her questions and letting the adults forget she was listening. This was especially true when Lana was one of the adults.

Lana and Aurora fed each other information carefully, as if they were dosing each other with strong medicine. Aurora talked about the wider world: There were huge machines that flew people around the world, and tiny ones that could keep a heart beating. Humans had walked on the moon. She described New York City, where more than eight million people lived. Eight million people.

Flattening one side of her ambergris with her thumb, Thea tried to hold the number in her mind. Eight rows of a million people. Eighty rows of one hundred thousand. Eight hundred rows of ten thousand.

Thea also learned that Lana had to beg Dolan to attend the first-line suppers, that she often had lunch with Lucian, and that she had all but given up hope for a baby. Neither of Thea's aunts talked about her mother, or about what might happen at Launch tomorrow.

After a couple of hours, Lana straightened up and said that the backways would be getting busy soon. They had to be careful about the hours they traveled. There was always the chance that Aurora would be discovered, even lying in the well of the sleigh with a blanket over her.

They were stepping into their furs when Aurora looked up as if she had just remembered something. "Lucian looks . . . he's so diminished."

Lana nodded without looking up, her face tight. "But he's better than he was, Aurora. He's so much better than he was. Dexna brought him back. Years, it took. He couldn't go back to teaching, but he's working again. He's nearly himself, sometimes."

Aurora shook her head. "When I think of how I last saw him. I've never forgotten the look on his face."

Lana glanced at Thea, who was doing her best to blend in among the ferns. "It's getting late," Lana said. "You two should be off. I'll be home for supper, Thea."

"No," Thea said. "I want to know what you two are talking about. Or aren't talking about."

Lana looked at her fingers. "All right." But she didn't seem to know where to start. "Did Lucian tell you anything about what happened after Rowen ordered . . . right before your mother and Aurora . . . left? For the surface?"

Aurora put her hand over Lana's. "Lucian met us at the tunnel. He had a vial of sealant, and he threatened Rowen with it. He said he would burn her if she didn't allow Mai to stay and be nursed in Gracehope. It was insane, desperate."

It was just the sort of thing someone *should* have done, Thea thought. "What did Rowen do?"

"Nothing," Lana said quietly. "Rowen didn't have to do anything, because Mai reached out and took the vial from Lucian's hand herself. She just reached out and took it, and then he kissed her." She turned to Aurora. "And then you and Mai were gone."

Thea drove Aurora back to the archive in silence. Lucian was outside with a sleigh and a team. She pulled her sleigh alongside his. "Good afternoon," he said, as if to the dogs. He was avoiding her eyes again, she thought. Or maybe it was Aurora he couldn't bear to see.

Aurora threw back her blanket and smiled at him. "Hello, Lucian. Are you coming or going?"

"In fact, I'm off to fetch Peter from the breeding grounds."

Thea offered to go instead. "Are you sure?" Aurora asked. "You've been ferrying us about all day."

"I'm very sure," Thea said. "I have to get Peg anyway." She also wanted to see if the runt had opened his eyes.

"Then I accept your kind offer." Lucian's eyes flickered over her face and then down again. It was a start.

Thea started along the quiet backways with her sleigh.

The pup's eyes are open, she chanted to herself, his eyes are open. Ten minutes later, her sleigh pulled up in front of the breeding grounds' double doors.

"Well?" she asked when she had knocked and Dolan peered out at her. But he just shook his head and let the door swing open.

She tried not to let him see her disappointment.

"There's still time," Dolan said quietly.

But not before tomorrow morning, Thea thought. *Not before Launch.* And then she realized that she was seeing the pup as a decoration that wouldn't be ready in time for her show. What was wrong with her? Dolan would never think about a dog that way.

She glanced around the main house. "Where's Peter?"

"Out there." He pointed.

She could just make out Peter's form against the glow of dimmed lightglobes. "He fell asleep?"

Dolan nodded. "Thought I'd leave him until someone came to get him."

Thea looked to where Mattias's companion, Ham, lay near Sasha in one of the stalls.

Dolan grunted. "Those two are nearly inseparable."

"Really? Do you . . . do you think we should . . . separate them? What if . . ."

Dolan looked at her. "I think it's none of our business. You'd better gather your cousin. He may take a minute to come to."

Thea stood over Cassie's box, where the pups and their mother had fallen asleep. She looked instinctively for the legend pup under Cassie's chin, but he wasn't there. She couldn't see him anywhere.

How could Cassie have fallen asleep without knowing her runt was safe? It wasn't like her. Anxiously, she felt among the bodies of the bigger pups; he must be tucked between two of them somewhere. No. She glanced to where Peter slept with his head resting on one arm.

And there, curled up under Peter's chin, was the legend pup.

THIRTY-FOUR

THEA

The next day, Thea woke early. She slipped out the dock door and ducked into the Chikchu shelter for a few minutes of comfort. Peg was already awake. Thea caressed her companion's ears absently, drawing strength from Peg's peacefulness. The Launch celebration would start in an hour, but she wasn't thinking about the passage, or Rowen, or any of that.

She was thinking about the runt. Thea couldn't help wondering about the night of his birth, of those long moments when he wasn't breathing, of the elation she had felt when he shuddered and finally took in air. Could she have done something differently?

A blind legend pup. Sela said that the rumors had already begun to circulate—something was wrong. For just a moment, she wondered whether the pup might truly be some sort of bad sign. Perhaps she never should have gone to the surface, or brought Peter back to Gracehope with her. What if things weren't supposed to change at all?

It was time to go back inside. She began to disentangle herself from Peg's warmth. Lynx, companion to Rowen, woke briefly just as Thea was getting to her feet. The dog raised his head sleepily.

Lynx began to signal, which was odd—he almost never addressed himself to Thea. The dog's thin noises rose and fell, his meaning weaving itself together slowly.

Swimwarm.

"Swimwarm" was the Chikchu signal for swimming in the lake. The water wasn't exactly warm, in truth, but that was what they called it. Thea had never met a Chikchu who didn't love to swim.

Swimwarm, Lynx signaled again. There was an air of self-congratulation about him: He closed his eyes in the slow blink the Chikchu used when they were satisfied.

Eyebrows raised hopefully, Peg turned to Thea. *Swimwarm?*

Thea shook her head before giving her companion a final kiss on the forehead. "No, love, not today."

Lana was just setting out breakfast. Dexna was next door having breakfast at home with Rowen. She said that nothing must appear out of the ordinary.

"I think Lynx could use some going out," Thea said. "The poor thing has an idea he's just been to the lake. Swimming, he says."

"At this hour?" Lana drew her chair to the table. "A dream, no doubt."

Mattias waited in front of his chambers alone. "My mother went ahead with Ezra," he said. "He insisted on skating. It will take him an age."

Arms and legs swinging in perfect rhythm, Thea and Mattias skated to the council chamber. Thea was nervous, but she felt more clear-minded than she had for a long time. There was no speech running through her head, no script. She skated with a sense of purpose that was much simpler than that, and was happy to have Mattias beside her.

Her calm evaporated when the lake came into view. Two engineering apprentices were posted near the tunnel entrance, their bright blue sashes visible from a distance. "*Mattias*," she said.

"Don't stop." He turned onto the lake path. "I'll catch up to you!"

She went slowly, and soon Mattias skated up beside her. "Gas escaping the fissure again," he explained breathlessly. "They were posted early this morning to make sure no one gets too close."

"Are you sure? Did you look at the . . . entrance?" Thea asked. She glanced around. There were a lot of people on the Mainway, all going to the Launch celebration.

"Just a quick look. But everything was just the same. Lucian repacked the wall very carefully. Don't worry." He gave her a broad smile as they took the last turn together, and then the council's courtyard was before them.

Though she had attended Launch every year of her life, Thea thought she had never seen the place so crowded. People were everywhere. They talked in small groups, mothers and uncles unpacking wrapped rice cakes and pieces of fruit for younger children. The Chikchu crowded around both sleigh docks and nestled together at the edges of the courtyard, where large water bowls had been set out for them. Among and around everyone, children darted, some already in costume, all giddy with excitement.

"Are you all right?" Mattias asked anxiously as they surveyed the crowd.

"I'm fine." Thea was trying to tug her sleeves down to her wrists. She should have worn a bigger fur.

"Let Launch begin!" someone called. The doors swung forward.

THIRTY-FIVE

PETER

Peter and his mother were at the breeding grounds, waiting for the others to return with news. Sasha had been fed and watered, and their sled stood packed and near the door, in case they had to leave quickly.

"You aren't going?" Peter asked Dolan. Mattias said that even Chief Berling, who hardly went anywhere, attended Launch every year. But Dolan shook his head. "No reason to go. But plenty of reasons to stay." He glanced around. "Look at this mess."

Peter's mother gave Dolan a long look. "It is rather

a mess," she said. "What you need is a proper apprentice."

He gave her a half-smile. "Perhaps you're right."

Peter helped Dolan clean the main house while his mother sat out on the sands with Norma, writing in her red notebook.

He saved Sasha's stall for last. "Hey, girl." He tickled her ears and laughed when she dropped and flipped over to have her belly rubbed.

Ham peered around the side of Sasha's stall, his expression so carefully nonchalant that Peter had to tell himself not to laugh. Never injure a Chikchu's dignity, Thea said.

After forking dog manure into a pile for later use in the gardens, Peter was ready for a walk. He washed up at the pump.

He was still tired from yesterday's training sessions with Dexna—she had insisted on another one after dinner—but his sight came a little more easily each time he tried it, and he knew that she deserved most of the credit. Thea said that he was getting off easy, that he had no idea how many hours she had spent learning the meanings of the Chikchus' signals. "It's like listening to a flute," she'd told him, "and having to translate into English."

He walked out to where his mom was sitting, the runt cradled in one hand while she wrote with the other. With a stab of worry, he recognized her glazed expression. Norma was stretched out alongside her, chin on her paws.

He sat down. "Still working on that?"

Half-asleep, Feet raised his head, staggered over to Peter's lap, and collapsed dramatically.

"He knows your voice." His mom laughed and snapped her notebook shut.

"I was thinking you could tell me about Launch," Peter said, "since I can't see the real thing, I mean."

She smiled slowly. "The real thing happened a long time ago. What's going on today is theater, a reenactment of the morning the Settlers escaped the old world. Younger children play all of the parts, and everyone has the morning off and goes to watch. It's a gruesome story, but you should know it, because the story of Launch is the story of William."

"And William is . . . ?"

"William was the last eye adept. Before you, I mean. He was the one who warned Grace that the hunters were coming."

Peter felt a sudden sense of foreboding.

She inhaled. "The story of Launch. The Settlers were almost ready to leave England for the cold world—Greenland, I mean. After years of preparation, Grace had two whaling ships chartered, along with everything they would need to settle their new land: tools, wood, plants and seeds, cloth, furs, medicines, books, enormous stockpiles of food, everything. They even had freshwater fish to stock the lake."

"They were pretending to hunt for whales?"

"Yes. Grace had posted some of her people to whaling crews for the past few years. They learned how to navigate a ship to Greenland."

"Smart," Peter said.

She nodded. "Grace tried not to take too many chances," she said. "But there was one risk she couldn't avoid. Grace had to trust outsiders to help with the launch itself. Every last one of her people was to board the ships to the cold world. She had a few trusted allies among the townsfolk, people who had helped them in the past.

"Before dawn, Grace and her people were collected at the docks. Their friends were to arrive soon to help them launch the ships. Grace had posted her eye adepts around the docks to watch for hunters. William was the youngest, about seventeen.

"What almost no one knew was that William was in love with one of the daughters of their allies. They had already said their private good-byes, but naturally he looked for her on the path. Finally, using his sight, he saw her walking toward the docks with her family, and crying.

"The crying didn't surprise him. What did surprise him was that at the girl's side was a dog William had never seen before. The girl's family had a number of dogs, but he couldn't place this one. It bothered him.

"He watched the girl and waited. A minute later, the dog raised its head quickly, as if barking. He saw the girl look over at the dog, and he realized that her expression wasn't one of sadness, but fear.

"William hesitated. To sound the call of alarm was a serious thing—it jeopardized everything, and what he had seen was possibly nothing. One dog, one bark, one look. But he had known this girl his entire life, and he loved her, and he was sure she was afraid.

"Grace accepted his judgment without question. She directed her people to abandon what was left of the supplies on the dock and to board just one of the ships. As the last of them was boarding, the hunters' dogs appeared, converging on the docks. Grace's allies had betrayed her.

"There was no time left. Grace jumped from the ship, and about ten others followed her down. They launched it themselves, pushing it off into the sea with what supplies it had. Then they turned to face the dogs.

"Sarah, Grace's granddaughter, was twelve years old. She watched from the deck of the ship as Grace was killed, along with others who had sacrificed themselves to launch the ship. That's why Grace never made it here.

But Sarah lived, and her children, and their children, and so on, down to us."

Peter shook his head. "They reenact this horror show every year?"

"Yes," his mother said. "The children adore it. Everyone wears costumes, and the betrayers march down the Mainway to the council's courtyard, and there's a big platform that serves as the dock. But it's not just a story, Peter. It's been a lesson to people here for a long time."

"A lesson that . . . what? The world is evil?"

His mother said nothing.

"What happened to William?"

"He was one of those who jumped down to launch the ship. He was killed by the dogs on the dock."

"Oh, that's good to hear," Peter said. "The self-sacrificing hero. He'll be an easy act to follow."

His mother looked at him. "Or maybe he was just a boy. And Peter, you aren't following anyone's act."

They were interrupted by Dolan. "Peter! Aurora!"

"Something's happened!" Peter's mother jumped up.

Peter gently replaced Feet in Cassie's whelping box and ran. His heart leapt when he saw that Dolan was standing in front of Sasha's stall.

But Sasha was in her usual corner, looking up at them peacefully. It was Ham who seemed to be in trouble. He was gagging, it looked like, throwing his head up violently and then lowering it, over and over, and making a

291

sound between a regular growl and something much more guttural.

"What's happening? Is he choking?" Peter looked at Dolan.

"No," Dolan said.

Ham's nose came almost to the ground and stayed there. He started to make a noise like a cat trying to get a hairball out of his throat. And then he threw up on the ground, right in front of Sasha.

"Oh, yuck," Peter said.

His mother wrapped her hand around his forearm. "Ham is telling us that he and Sasha have mated. He's offering to provide for her, to be her partner."

"What?"

Sasha stood up and sniffed what Ham had left on the ground.

"Double yuck," Peter said. His mother's hand stayed on his arm.

Sasha turned and then lay down again, her hindquarters to Ham.

"And she accepts him," his mother said. She and Dolan began talking at the same time.

Sasha wasn't coming to New York, Peter realized. A sudden heat in his chest told him how hard he had been holding on to that piece of happiness. He watched as Ham took his place next to Sasha, and then he walked back out to the sands feeling numb.

Norma was curled up asleep, a soft mound of black fur. Peter settled himself next to her. If only they had left yesterday, he thought. He and Sasha would be safely back in the geebee geebee now.

There was a flash of gray and white behind Norma. Peter peered over the dog's flank and saw Feet making his way toward him. He glanced at Cassie's whelping box across the sand—the pup had come a long way.

"Hey, Feet," he said. "How did you find your way over here?" He reached out to rub the dog behind the ears. Feet tipped his face with pleasure.

Peter's hand stopped. "Feet! You did it!" He scooped up the pup. "We don't have a whole lot of time. Let's see if Dolan will give us a ride."

"No." Peter's mom stood in front of the locked doors with her arms crossed. "It isn't safe."

"But Mom, I want to do this! It's important. I'm sick of hiding out!"

Something flashed across his mother's face then, and her eyes darted over his head. Peter turned and found Dolan behind him.

"I'll keep him safe, Aurora. You have my word."

She smiled and looked like she was about to cry at the same time.

"All right."

Peter meant for all of them to go together. But his

mom said, "I'll stay with the Chikchu. This is for you to do, I think. And I have something to finish before we leave this afternoon."

Peter glared at the red notebook in her hands and turned to Dolan.

"Let's be off, then." Dolan slid back the lock on the doors.

THIRTY-SIX

THEA

Inside the council chamber, the stage was set: There was the long shipping dock, dyed carefully to look like real wood, and, a bit higher up, the two whaling ships' decks—one to the left and one to the right. Woven ladders hung down from each ship to the dock, which was piled with boxes and baskets.

Red banners hung everywhere, and a few old-world houses painted onto slabs of sealed ice leaned against the walls. Lightglobes blazed. The chamber was packed with people, some with young children on their shoulders.

High above everyone's heads, the icy forms of the Settlers continued their endless march.

Thea and Mattias sank into their seats on the balcony between Dexna and Lucian. Rowen sat on her podium opposite them, wearing a dark red cloak. The sight of her grandmother ignited something inside Thea.

Rowen called the celebration to order, and the chamber quieted. The boy who played the part of William always took the stage first, and Thea watched along with everyone else to see who it would be this year.

A smallish boy in an old-world costume appeared nervously at the back of the stage and began walking forward, to quick applause. She remembered the year Mattias had won the part of William—he hadn't been able to eat a thing that morning.

The girl playing Grace was now taking her place on the dock, and then other children in costume appeared, climbing onto the stage. They made themselves busy with the boxes and baskets, carrying them down the dock and then passing them up to the ships' decks. The parcels had words written on them, "seeds" or "ink" or "medicine." Thea had loaded this same cargo several times when she was young enough to participate in Launch—her middling school marks had never earned her a more distinguished role.

Grace slowly walked over to William, who looked ready to collapse in anxiety.

"Oh, poor thing," Thea whispered to Mattias.

"Our friends should be here soon," said Grace. Her volume was impressive, though she couldn't have been more than ten. "You and the other eye adepts keep watch."

William just nodded.

There was a murmur—everyone in the chamber knew that William was supposed to say his line: "Yes, Grace, and I will alert you if I see hide or hair of the hunters." He was also supposed to wipe his eyes, because he was bereft at having to leave his secret love in the old world. Thea began to hope that Dexna would get on with their plan, if only to save the boy further embarrassment.

Dexna must have read her mind. She stood up and spoke in a voice that filled the chamber. "We all know what happens next, don't we?"

Every face on the floor turned up to the balcony, shock written on most of them—no one had heard Dexna speak for fifteen years. Rowen's expression was grim, but far from surprised.

"I do apologize for the interruption," Dexna continued. "But I don't imagine that anyone will find the suspense too difficult to bear. Grace's friends betray her in this chamber year after year, do they not? Perhaps it is time for another story."

She turned to Thea, whose mind buzzed and went entirely blank at the same time. "Me?" she whispered. Dexna took her hand and brought her to her feet.

"My niece, Thea, is not distinguished by grades or apprenticeship. But there is something that marks her as different: She has shown the courage to reach out where she was taught to shrink back in fear."

Dexna sat, leaving Thea to stand alone.

Everyone looked confused, or stunned. But Dexna had given her the floor.

"Friends," she said. "I have been to the surface."

Thea believed that the chamber was silent when she opened her mouth to speak. But she had been wrong: There must have been fifty hushed conversations taking place, complaints of hunger from children, murmurs about Dexna. Now they stopped. Even the children seemed to stop breathing.

Rowen exploded. "Do not heed this girl!"

Thea kept her eyes on the people below. "The Settlers themselves preserved the passage to the surface. They left it for us deliberately. And Rowen has known of it!"

Rowen's voice was a growl. "On my line, Thea, you will—"

Thea forced herself to meet her grandmother's burning eyes. "It is my line now, Rowen, isn't that so? I am the last bearing daughter of the first line, and without my daughters, there will be no more of it."

Rowen was nearly suffocated by rage. "What of Grace?" She pointed to the carved figure above them.

"What do you say to those who sacrificed for the way of life you cast off?"

"Grace never intended this to be our way of life forever!" Thea shouted.

People started talking; some looked angry. Angry at Thea. Rowen smiled. She raised her eyebrows. "Grace didn't intend this?" Rowen swept her arms in front of her. "A beautiful world full of healthy people?"

Thea looked down at the people below. "Yes—no! Not forever. Her true hope was that this world could shelter us until we were ready to return to the surface." She noticed Lana in the crowd below; the Angus stood next to her.

"I see. And you have decided that the time has come, have you? A girl of ten and four."

Thea's heart sank. It sounded ridiculous even to her.

"Have you known of the passage, Rowen?" Chief Berling was not a talkative man, but everyone knew his voice, and the chamber hushed. "Is this true?"

Thea looked at Rowen, daring her to lie.

Rowen said nothing.

"Answer me!" Berling bellowed.

"Of course I have known of it!" Rowen cried. "It is a passage to brutality, to sickness, to death, and it has been my job to protect every life here from entering it! My own daughter, Mai, discovered the passage. She threatened our world with her own curiosity and finally destroyed herself! Now Mai's daughter, my granddaughter, tries to do the same." Rowen doubled over, sobbing.

Thea was stunned. She had never seen this sort of emotion from Rowen. Perhaps Rowen *was* truly afraid; maybe she loved Mai and had hated to give her up. As much as she despised her grandmother, a part of her wanted to believe.

It was almost a minute before Rowen collected herself. "Mai did not drown," she said, sniffling.

Silence. Thea waited.

"My daughter visited the wider world without anyone's knowledge, and she contracted an illness there. We did all we could, despite what she had done to hurt us, despite the risk to ourselves. But there was no way to save her. She died in my arms."

Her grandmother's words gave Thea the sort of shock that wipes every thought from the mind. She didn't hear the sympathetic gasp from the chamber, and she didn't see that Lucian had risen to his feet beside her.

One memory floated up to her: She remembered holding her mother's locket up for her grandmother on Ezra's birthday. Rowen was bothered more by Thea's chewed fingernails than by the memory of her own lost daughters.

Then Lucian exploded. "No way to save her? There was no *attempt* to save her! Mai was a sacrifice, Rowen. A sacrifice to your fear! You cast her out! She didn't die in your arms, but on the surface! What a foul liar you are. You don't care for the people here, any more than you did for your own daughter. You care only for a way of life over which you have great control! You were afraid of Mai, of where she might lead our people!"

"Of course I was afraid!" Rowen cried. "I was afraid for all of us. Afraid of what Mai's selfishness would bring upon Gracehope. Do you think I would have parted with a daughter, had I any choice?"

Rowen was painting the story as her own terrible sacrifice. Thea felt hot and dizzy. She was afraid she might be sick.

Lucian yelled out across the crowd, his neck bright red, the tendons standing out clearly. "She is deceiving you—Mai could have been saved! Rowen did have a choice!"

No more than a handful of people looked up at him, and those who did looked reproachful. Thea had never felt so helpless: She told the truth about the passage, about Grace's real hopes for their people, and somehow none of it made a difference. She stared, numb.

Rowen shook her head. "No, Lucian. I had no more choice than I do today. There are engineering apprentices posted at the passage right now, with strict instructions that no one is to come near the lake."

Lucian started yelling again. Thea's thoughts began to collect themselves.

Swimwarm.

~~Lynx *had* been~~ to the lake before first light this morning. Rowen must have gone to inspect the passage wall; perhaps she suspected something. Then she needed only to tell Chief Berling that she had seen gas escaping the fissure in the lakebed. He would have posted his apprentices there within the quarter hour. It was so simple. She wanted to scream. Everything Dexna feared had come true—Thea appeared young and foolish, Lucian looked like a lunatic, and the passage was out of reach. Rowen would surely seal the entrance this time. Aurora and Peter would be trapped forever. She looked at Dexna, who sat perfectly still with her eyes on the crowd below and a smile creeping across her face. Was she insane?

Thea followed Dexna's gaze to the chamber floor. In the midst of all those huddled heads, someone was waving at her. It was Peter, making his way in from the great doors. And Dolan was right in front of him, clearing a path through the crowd.

Lucian fell silent. People had begun to notice Peter, whose yellow hair glowed among the dark heads. In another moment the chamber was quiet.

Peter stopped right below Thea and smiled at her. He gestured at the crook of his arm. The runt! He swept the tiny dog up over his head.

The pup's eyes were open, and they were blue. Sky blue.

The runt's four white feet dangled in the air. Thea

302

heard a young man say, "The pup! Look at the pup he's got."

Someone said "The legend pup!" and the chamber was ringing with voices.

"Who is that?"

"It's true!"

"And he *can* see—"

"Who is that boy?"

"Look at his hair!"

"Everyone," Thea called over the noise, "I would like to introduce my cousin. His name is Peter. He has come here from the wider world."

The room fell silent.

"Hello." Peter held the runt tightly as he nodded at the people around him. "Nice to meet you." His neighbors were frozen. Thea saw him take a tiny step toward Dolan.

Children on shoulders pointed at Peter, and people stood on tiptoe to see him. They found their voices again, and everyone talked at once. Thea felt a quick chill. Several things could fall into place now, if she did things right. The way Rowen would, perhaps.

"Peter is an eye adept," Thea said evenly. "The first born to our people since William."

"Nonsense," Rowen snapped. "There are no eye adepts among us anymore."

"There is one now." Thea smiled. "One who was raised in the wider world."

"Raised by whom?" Rowen flashed.

"By my mother!" Peter said. "Her name is Aurora. And by my father, Gregory."

Aurora. The name swept the hall.

Rowen's face was stony. "In Gracehope we do not speak of those who take their own lives," she said severely.

"My mother didn't take her own life!" Peter told her angrily. "She's at the breeding grounds right now." At this, the voices rose again.

Rowen looked around. "The boy is not an adept. William was the last eye adept, sent to us to provide safe passage to Gracehope. This boy is an intruder."

Peter turned to face Rowen. She was *his* grandmother, too, Thea realized. "I *am* an eye adept," he said, though with less conviction. Thea saw him glance nervously at Dexna next to her on the balcony, but Dexna made no move to help him.

"Boy!" A woman's voice came from the far side of the chamber. "Boy! Tell me what is in my hand." A figure raised an arm in the distance.

Peter turned toward the voice, and the crowd pressed back so that his line of sight was clear. Peter stood still as a stone, his yellow hair pointing in three directions and the hood of his fur bunched up inside his collar. No one in the chamber seemed to breathe.

"It's a cloth doll," Peter said finally. "With black hair, and a dirty blue dress."

"That's right!" the voice called out, and the chamber broke into loud talk.

"A trick!" Rowen spat. "They've tricked you!"

Another voice rang out from the far side of the chamber, silencing everyone: "Tell me, Peter. What is at my throat?" It was the Angus.

Peter froze again, and then said, "It's a red ribbon, and there's something hanging from it . . . a circle, with three little bars across it. They're . . . wavy."

He was describing the water sign of the twelfth bloodline: the Angus's bloodline.

"The child is an adept, Rowen," the Angus called.

Rowen colored. "This boy is not one of us," she said, "and he may very well infect any who touch him, just as Mai was sickened in the wider world. None of us is safe with him here among us."

The people closest to Peter looked at one another and then, more closely, at him. They didn't move any nearer, but they didn't step away either.

Rowen was down off her podium and striding toward Peter, her eyes on the pup. She thrust out her hands. "You are a danger to us, and you are a danger to the Chikchu you hold. Give it to me before you sicken it." She reached into Peter's arms, and grasped the pup with one hand.

"Better not," Dolan said.

The pup's mouth opened in silent protest. Silent to

305

some. Thea heard it—it was a tiny shriek, like the noise a baby might make watching his mother walk away. The other ear adepts in the room probably heard it as well. And so did all of the Chikchu waiting in the courtyard.

In the next moment, the air was full of long, sharp howls. The dogs' cries pierced and echoed, crisscrossing layers of sound that made thought impossible. It was unbearable. Children put their hands over their ears and squeezed their eyes shut. The adults looked scared.

Dolan stood in the middle of the crowd, looking pointedly at Rowen, who was dangling the pup by one hand, a look of pure shock on her face. Peter reached out and clutched the pup back to his chest. The howling stopped.

Dolan laid a hand on Peter's shoulder. "The boy and the dog are together now."

Rowen looked at Dolan with blazing eyes and stalked back to her high podium.

"Grandmother," Thea started, "no one here seeks to end our way of life, only our fear of the world above us. That was Grace's hope. Her hope was that we might choose for ourselves how to live. Here, or on the surface."

"Choose?" Rowen roared. "That choice has been made!"

The chamber erupted in protest, and Rowen found herself shouted down every time she attempted to speak. She waved to the crowd for quiet and pointed across the chamber to Thea. "She is my daughter's daughter, but it is time to show this child that we will not allow the one to sacrifice the many. We will not permit the dangerous impulse of a thoughtless girl to risk the lives of all of our children. Turn your back to her now, and we will set to work together. We will preserve what Grace built for us!"

Thea shouted: "It is you who betray Grace, Rowen. You have forced ignorance upon us, and encouraged our fear. I promise you this: The first line is finished seeking refuge. Sons or daughters, my children will know the stars."

There was a collective intake of breath. She felt Mattias turn to look at her.

One woman, a mother holding a child, spoke up in a loud clear voice.

"Only one speaks the truth, Rowen. I don't believe it is you."

And she turned her back to Rowen and faced Thea, who recognized her from the gardens, where she was a caretaker. She looked steadily at Thea while her son wound his fingers in his mother's hair.

Another woman turned toward Thea, showing Rowen her back, and then her brother did the same. Thea stood, struck dumb, as a murmuring rose from one corner of the room and then another, and more and more people turned their backs to Rowen, who stood with an eerie calm.

"Fools!" she said. "You look to a child for wisdom! She

seeks to waste the lives of the ancients who gave themselves to find this refuge for our people! She would lead you back into a world of cruelty for no reason other than her own childish curiosity!"

A group of cousins from the third line turned to face Thea. Then more people. And more. She acknowledged each, her mind spinning.

Every face in the room was looking up at her.

THIRTY-SEVEN

PETER

When Peter got back to the breeding grounds with Dolan, his mother was asleep on the sands with Norma keeping watch over her. The red notebook was lying open. She was almost to the last page. He hovered over the book, unable to stop himself from looking.

He read:

Mai was on the narrow sleigh, her small body wrapped in blankets and furs. Her color was high, which was strange—she'd been so pale lately—and with wisps of hair escaping the fur hood that I had pulled up over her ears, she looked young and healthy—a bit tired, perhaps, as if she'd spent the afternoon skating.

Norma and Gru pulled the sleigh. Gru knew the passage well by this time and had taken up her customary pace. Mai fell asleep almost immediately, Lucian's sealant tube still clutched in one hand. Despite her sickness and exhaustion, Mai seemed able to sense the air of the wider world— she always said she could hear it—and she roused just as I was turning the sleigh toward Gregory's camp.

There was a high wall of ice that marked the way—I loved the way it changed color in the light—rose one morning, blue/gray the next afternoon. It looked like many other ice ridges nearby, and Mai had always marked her way with one of her bracelets, unclasping the braided ring from her arm as she approached the ice wall and driving it into the grainy surface with one hand as she passed, never stopping the dogs. It was her trailmark, to be reclaimed on her way back home. Later, when the land became familiar to her, she had no need of it, but the act had come to feel natural, a clap of greeting on the shoulder of an old friend.

Now, as we passed the wall, Mai reached out a hand to feel its rough surface, wondering, I imagined, that she had ever had such casual strength.

"Stop."

Although there was a slight wind and Mai's voice was weak, I heard the word clearly—I had been listening for it. I stood with the dogs and watched as Mai unclasped one bracelet and drew her arm back.

The bracelet hardly broke the first layer of ice crystals that clung to the wall, but for the moment it stayed where Mai had placed it, much to my relief. I hoped to move on before the bracelet dropped to the ground, but she opened the tube of sealant and threw the contents of the flask at her bracelet. The ice around it cleared until the bracelet appeared to be suspended in midair.

The bracelet, woven strands of spun ice dyed the color of blood, seemed to pulse with color in the bright sunlight, as if it had been somehow animated rather than frozen in place for earth's eternity.

I cried, looking at it, not because I knew that Mai would never again see her trailmark, although I did know that, but because I understood that, however hard I might try, her memory could never be preserved as purely.

Peter reached out and closed the notebook, realizing as he touched it that he had actually hated the thing. He'd half-believed it was taking his mother away. But it was just an ordinary red notebook, with two words written on the cover now: *For Thea*.

He glanced over to where his mother lay next to Norma, and was surprised to find her watching him, her head propped up on one hand.

She smiled. "So, what happened?"

An hour later Peter waited in the main house while his mother, Dolan, Lana, and Thea huddled around Cassie's whelping box out on the sands. He resisted the urge to use his sight to spy on them. Instead, he watched Sasha, who had fallen asleep in a corner of her stall. In a little while he would be saying good-bye. He tried to form a permanent picture of her in his mind.

Dolan came toward him. "Ready?"

Peter nodded. They walked toward the whelping box, where Thea stood solemnly with one hand on Cassie's head. When Peter stopped in front of her, she gave him a short bow, and then reached down to where Feet sat next to his mother. Thea gathered the pup into her hands.

"I give you Feet," she said, holding him out to Peter, "your one companion."

Peter took Feet and held him. He gave Thea a little bow, and then he bowed to Cassie, too. "Thank you."

Dolan smiled broadly. Peter's mother was crying.

"Now what?" Peter whispered to Thea.

Thea grinned. "Now you take care of each other."

He wished he could take Feet home today. But Dolan said Feet needed to spend a few more weeks with his mother first.

The call sounded from the main house, and a few moments later Sela and Mattias were walking out to meet them. Dolan hadn't bothered to bolt the doors.

"I found them!" Sela called. With one hand, she waved a pair of skates.

"Mattias outgrew them a year ago," she said breathlessly. "And is this your little man?" She peered at Feet. "Pretty one, he is. The legend pup—still hard to believe."

Peter rubbed the pup's head, and Feet batted at his hand with one paw. "Or maybe he's just a dog." He put Feet in the whelping box. "You watch out for him, okay, Cassie? Don't let anyone squish him."

Thea laughed. "He'll be fine. And soon he'll be all yours."

The skates fit perfectly. Peter took a few practice runs on the pass in front of the breeding grounds. Then he gave Sasha a long hug.

Thea, Mattias, and Peter set out for the Mainway together. It was nearly suppertime now, and lightglobes burned a deep green outside the doors they passed. The Mainway was busy, and Peter knew that people were noticing him. Most of them skated alone, or in twos. There were some boys carrying giant bags of bread, and one with an orange sash who skated by so fast Peter's knees went weak for a moment.

"Messenger," Thea said to him. "They're a bit showy."

He caught someone's eye, a woman's, and smiled at her. She smiled back. But for the most part, he concentrated on making the turns without knocking anyone over. The path split a few times, wound to the left, then to the right, then left again. Thea and Mattias led the way, leaning into their strides without seeming to think about it. For every step they took, it felt like he took four. But he was elated.

And then the lake came into view. The water was still, reflecting the low light and the branches of the trees around it. Thea and Mattias stopped at the lake path and bent down to their skates. He leaned over and flipped his blades up to the sides of his boots the way Sela had shown him.

They waited for the others. No one talked—it was one of those times when you felt like you had to say something really important or nothing at all. He would have to have Miles make up a word for that.

"Here they come," Thea said.

A minute later, Dolan and Sela pulled up on a sleigh, with Lana and Peter's mom right behind them on the sled Peter had taken from camp two days before. His mom held her red notebook under one arm. She got out, untied the team of dogs, and pulled the sled onto the lake path. They all trooped down the path toward the tunnel, not talking.

Dexna and Lucian were waiting there. The entrance to the passage was much wider than before—a person could walk through it standing up now. And there were a couple of lightglobes resting on the ground on either side of it. It looked almost like a door.

Dexna walked up to Peter. "We have an appointment, then?"

"A week from today. And I'll remember to practice."

Sela pulled a stiff folder from a bag at her feet. "There was hardly any time for it, but I wanted you to have this now." She took a single sheet of paper from the folder. It was a drawing of Sasha.

Peter nodded, his throat tight.

"And this is for you, Thea." His mom pressed her red notebook into Thea's hands.

"Thank you," Thea looked at the cover and fingered the metal spiral. "But what is it?"

His mom looked like she was going to cry. "It's everything I wish I had been able to tell you, about your mother."

Thea smiled and hugged the book to her.

Sela put one arm around Mattias and the other around Thea. "Losh, it's only a sevennight," she said. "Be off with you!"

And then Peter and his mother were walking up the passage together, pulling the sled behind them.

They emerged blinking into the brightness of the late afternoon sun. Peter looked toward camp, allowing himself to draw the sight closer. The geebee geebee stood there, and Jonas's igloo, and the dogs' shelter, and the research tent. Nothing had changed.

When Peter and his mom trudged up the slope to the camp, Peter's father was just coming out of the research tent with an armful of equipment. He began to run: If Peter had looked closely enough, he would have seen tiny pins flying in every direction, drill parts dropped, a heavy battery disappearing into the snow with no sound at all. Arms open, Dr. Solemn launched himself at Peter and his mother.

And then they were all falling.

"Ouch! Goodness, Gregory!"

They had landed in one of Jonas's snow pits.

The next day, Dr. Solemn assigned Jonas a long day of pit-digging. Peter and his parents sat in the geebee geebee and talked.

"How much longer will they be safe down there?" Peter asked. "Before the ice melts, or cracks?"

"I wish I knew," his dad said. "Twenty years? Maybe more."

"But maybe less?"

"It's possible."

"Where will they go?"

"There's plenty of time to talk about that," Peter's mother said. "To England, perhaps. We'll have to see what we can do." She glanced at Peter's dad. "An international effort."

He nodded, then smiled at her. "We won't be able to sneak them out under a blanket in a Cessna, that's for sure. That worked for you, but—"

"No." Peter's mom shook her head. "No more hiding."

Jonas hadn't asked questions when Peter and his mother returned to camp, not even about Sasha. He'd just asked if Peter felt like experimenting with the cookie mix. "I'm getting tired of the same ones over and over. I was thinking we could whip up some oatmeal-chip brownies or something."

A few days later, Peter and Jonas were lying in the igloo eating their most recent experiment: banana-butterscotch bars.

"So," Jonas said. "I guess your parents found whatever it was they were looking for."

Peter watched clouds pass overhead through the hole in the roof. "I was looking for it, too," he said. "I just didn't know."

Jonas laughed. "Happens to me all the time."

Their last weeks in Greenland continued in a happier version of what had gone on before. Peter's headaches were gone. His mom sat on her bed and began to write her book on mitochondrial DNA. She'd decided to include a short history of a family that fled England centuries ago. She couldn't help Thea get Gracehope ready for the world, she said, but she could help the world get ready for Gracehope.

Peter's dad had sent away for some radio-building kits, and he and Peter drove the dogsled to the post office in Qaanaaq to pick them up, along with a bunch of up-to-date world maps and history books.

There was also a letter from Miles:

> Dear Peter:
>   Arms bigger than ever.
> Evil stepsisters plotting to decorate
> my room like tikki hut.
> Awaiting your advice.
>
>   Miles (away)
>
> P.S. How goes the ice cube-island thing?
> P.P.S. Why haven't you written????

Peter kept his first appointment with Dexna, going down the tunnel with an armful of maps and books to find her waiting at the bottom. And then there were other appointments. On days that Jonas and Dr. Solemn spent in the field, Peter and his mother slipped away. And each time Peter approached the ring in the ice wall, his longing for Gracehope nearly overcame him. He realized that he had grown to be like his mother after all: From now on, his heart would live in two places. Or maybe three.

Then it was their last week in Greenland: The days that once stretched out before him were all but gone. Jonas went south to his grandparents' village, where he would spend the summer. He peeled his name from the back of his chair and slid it carefully into his backpack. "I can't remember how many kitchen chairs they have," he explained. "I want to be prepared." He also took all the pancake and brownie mix. That afternoon, Peter and his mother brought Feet back to camp.

It was cloudy the day the Air National Guard plane came back for them. Peter tucked Feet inside his parka.

The pilot waved his paper cup of cold coffee at the geebee geebee. "If it weren't for that blue monster, I wouldn't have been able to land. Can't tell the ice from the clouds today," he said. "You leaving it there?"

"Yes," said Dr. Solemn. "We'll be needing it again."

THIRTY-EIGHT

THEA

EIGHT MONTHS LATER

Holidays were observed quietly in Gracehope. "Imagine every line trying to put a feast like this on their greatroom table on the same night," Sela said to Thea, eyeing the platters. "The lake would be empty and the plants stripped down to nothing." But births were rare enough to be celebrated with abandon.

Mattias crammed another sweetroll into his mouth.

"Those aren't all for you, Mattias!" Sela called. "At least wait until the guests begin to arrive. And you might bring one or two rolls to Lana. She's in with the baby."

Thea was not the last bearing daughter of the first line after all. Lana had a daughter, Iris.

"I'll take them to her," Thea said. She put a few rolls on a plate along with some sliced fruit.

"Oh, thank heavens!" I haven't had a chance to eat all morning!" Lana popped a sweetroll into her mouth. She looked beautiful, as always, though since the baby there was often something disheveled about her—a missed button or a falling-out hair comb. Today her sash was coming undone. Thea retied it while Lana ate.

Iris was lying on Lana's bed, gurgling happily under a fur blanket and waving her arms over her head. Beside her was a little pile of baby clothes.

"I was trying to dress her," Lana said with her mouth full. "But she won't stop moving."

Thea untied the red ribbon that held her locket. "I-ris," she sang. "I-ris. Time to get dressed for your party." She swung the locket gently over the baby's head. Iris immediately dropped her arms and tried to focus on it, her eyes nearly crossed with the effort. Lana had her dressed in a minute.

"What am I going to do without you, Thea?"

"I'm not going anywhere for months!" Thea laughed. "And then I'll be gone for only a fortnight!"

Lana hoisted Iris to her shoulder. "It will be impossible to bear."

The surface expeditions would be starting in the spring. Thea was to go with the Chikchu teams as Dolan's apprentice. She had already begun to make the dogs special coats so they wouldn't freeze the way Ham and Peg had. In time, she would breed Sasha's thick-coated pups into a line of dogs better-suited for the cold world.

In a few months, Peter and Aurora would be back, and they would all start to plan. Not many people in Grace-hope knew that the cold world was warming: Chief Berling did, of course, and a few others. One step at a time, Dexna said. First, let people enjoy the sunlight. Aurora said that Peter's father would teach Berling and a few apprentices how to recognize signs that the ice was breaking up; Mattias had asked to be one of them.

Back in the greatroom, Thea helped Lana at the counter while Mattias hovered protectively over the tray of sweetrolls. Lucian appeared in the doorway. He had started to visit occasionally, usually with something he thought Thea might like to read. Often the books were hopelessly boring—an old treatise on botany or geology. But she liked seeing him.

"Thea!" Sela called from a gift-covered table. "I need this cleared for more food, if you can comprehend it. Can you take these things to your chamber?"

It seemed that every family in Gracehope had sent something over, no matter how chipped or tattered. Thea dumped everything on her bed. A few things slipped to the floor, including a toy ricewater pot. It had no top, and there were two stones wedged in the bottom of it. Thea sat down with the pot in her hands. She had no memory of the thing, but she believed what Lana told her, that she had loved it once.

She put two fingers into it, feeling the smooth, unmoving stones, and looked at the picture that hung above her trunk. It showed her mother and Aurora, in the sunlight. A photograph, Peter had called it. Aurora had sent it down the tunnel with the Chikchu after Mai died, and Sela had kept it hidden all these years.

Lana appeared in the doorway. "Dexna's arrived. Are you through here?"

Dexna had been elected Chief of Council shortly after Launch. It was difficult for Thea to remember her as a quiet person, let alone a silent one.

Thea held out the pot in her hands. "Look what I found."

Lana laughed. "Goodness! Are the stones still there?"

"Yes." Thea showed her. "Lana, do you remember what Dexna said about me at Launch? How I had the courage to reach out where I had been taught to be afraid?"

Her aunt came and sat on the bed next to her. "Of course I do."

"It's not true. Mattias was hopelessly wedged in the ice, and I saw Peter and Sasha. But I didn't call out to them."

"You must have," Lana said.

"No, I didn't," Thea said. "It was Gru who called them. I just closed my eyes and hoped they would be gone when I looked again. If Gru hadn't started shrieking, Mattias would have died, and nothing . . . nothing would have changed."

Lana stood. "It was natural to be afraid. Gru was able to push you past your fear. The Chikchu have been our guides for a long time, Thea. Mai liked to say that's why we name them for the stars." She held out a hand. "We're going to have a toast to your little sister. Ready?"

"Is Rowen here?" Thea had only glimpsed her grand-mother a few times since Launch. Dexna said she rarely left her chamber.

Lana shook her head. "No, she hasn't come. I didn't expect her to—she's as stubborn as the stones in that pot."

"Then why did you invite her?"

Lana smiled. "Because she's my mother. And I suppose I'll keep inviting her for the same reason."

Thea rose, set the ricewater pot on her bed, and fol-lowed Lana to where the others waited.

"It's real tea," Mattias said as they took their cups from a tray. He stood grinning with Dexna, Sela, Ezra, and Dolan. Thea noticed that he had two more sweetrolls in his free hand. Sela held Iris, who was asleep. Lucian hovered outside the family circle, looking down into his glass.

Dolan cleared his throat. "To Iris's daughters!" The traditional toast at the birth of a daughter.

Thea raised her glass. With her other arm, she pulled Lucian into the group. "But first, to Iris. May she be brave enough to take the rightful path, and fortunate enough to have friends who can help her to see it."

And they drank.

EPILOGUE

PETER

Peter lay in bed and watched through the skylight as darkness fell. Feet was sprawled over his legs.

"Ouch. Feet, can you move?"

The big dog picked his head up and panted happily.

"Please? My legs are numb."

More happy panting.

"Okay. You win." Peter spread the fingers of one hand and tapped the palm of the other: *Food.*

Feet rocketed off the bed and down the coat-closet

stairs. A second later, Peter heard his mother laugh in the kitchen downstairs. "Again? You eat more than the rest of us together!"

"Any special requests, Peter?" She called. "I'm ordering dinner from Mama Foo's."

Feet was practically addicted to moo shu chicken.

"Just the usual. Don't forget, Miles is sleeping over!" The lights in the windows across the street began to blink on, but Peter looked beyond them, to the sky. If it stayed clear, he would be able to see the stars later. Real ones. He'd been practicing.

Miles rang the doorbell five minutes after the food arrived. He sniffed the air suspiciously. "We're not having Chinese food, are we?"

"Of course we are! It's Friday."

"But Feet always farts after Chinese!"

Peter laughed. "I'll turn on the fan."

They were up in the loft getting ready for bed when Peter's dad came home. He had lots of meetings these days.

"Pete!" his father called. "Postcard from Jonas!" Jonas was doing fieldwork in Colorado. The card came flying in over the loft railing from the living room. Feet ran for it, but Peter got there first.

The front of the card was a picture of a Volkswagen, a

sporty one. Peter flipped it over: *Next time we'll find it.* He smiled and propped it up on his shelf next to Sela's sketch of Sasha and the blue golf ball Jonas had sent him for Christmas.

Miles unrolled his sleeping bag. "I still don't get why they call it Greenland. I'm going to think of something better."

Peter looked through the skylight and thought of all the words he wished he could share with Miles: lightglobe, Chikchu, Mainway, eye adept. The night sky glowed faintly. Feet jumped up and draped himself over Peter's legs.

Miles was still talking. " 'Iceland' is taken, obviously. How about 'Snowland'?"

"Sounds like a Christmas display at Macy's," Peter mumbled. "The Greenlanders call it 'human's land.' "

"Human's land? But that could be anywhere."

Peter held still and drew the stars down to him until a blanket of lights seemed to shine softly just over his head. "You're right," he said. "It could be anywhere."

My deepest thanks to J. Alison James, Karen Romano Young, and my editor, Wendy Lamb, for their encouragement, insight, and tireless scrutiny of my many drafts. I am also obliged to Robert Warren, Ruth Homberg, and Faye Bender for their advice and penetrating questions. And I'm very grateful for my nonadult readers: Anika James, Kye and Ivo Lippold, and Marissa Keller.

I owe a special debt to Konrad Steffen, director of the Cooperative Institute for Research in Environmental Sciences at the University of Colorado, who corresponded with me so generously about arctic fieldwork. Any error or embellishment is, of course, my own doing.